TRESSPASS INTO EVIL

Tresspass Into Evil

Brenda C Dontcha

Brenda Calen Dontcha

12345 Range Road 1&1/2
Tropical Island, South Pacific
1-098-765-4321

Feel free to pop by and visit any time, the Komodo dragons like a good neck
scratch. Don't worry about calling first, just drop in.
© Brenda Calen Dontcha

ISBN 978-0-9685835-3-1
November 2024

Dedication

To Mom

She Knows why.

Yes, but the readers don't.

"Is that really important?"

You know it is.

"I mea.., shit, okay, fine, damnations!"

LANGUAGE!

"Ooopsie!"

Just get on with it already!

"Okay, okay! I'll express myself in greater detail, if I have to, I guess..."

Dedicated to My Mother, were our situations reversed, I believe I may not have been. She was strong enough to do all that was needed to make sure I existed, then went on with all the other needs. The only uncertainty when it comes to my gratitude,
"Can it be measured."

I am grateful.

Prologue

I believe there are two kinds of warriors walking this earth. Those that look for the fray. Then there are those like myself, those who strive to avoid it. And even when that proves to be non-viable, I will always strive to not overindulge in such an appetizing scenario. I am Colleen, I travel at the behest of the cosmos and do not question the journeys laid out before me. I will continue on as I always have. Whether this uncompromising doctrine of mine means more life or that I am meant to be sent off to the next one. I won't reason why.

1

I'm just another bleeder walking this earth. I always liked words. Especially those that could take me back to era's prior to the modern times in which I strive to tolerate. When the etymology of a word could transp...

"YOU'RE FUCKIN' DEAD, BITCH!"

"Ah, another small country being heard from." Colleen muttered as she continued rummaging through her rucksack.

He's a country, all right – emphasis on the c, the u and lose the o, r and y. He really was, she thought. No means no and then to attempt to get violent when the object of your desire rebuffs. I guess, in this case and regarding other prior situations, maybe I'm not a complete schmuck. Not the first time I've left someone in an embarrassing state of affairs for others to find. It's not my job to sort the garbage, fate just keeps asking me to take out the trash, Colleen pondered. I'm just hitching rides and end up defying the odds of having more than several encounters with such embarrassments to the human race. One of them was female, my goodness, was she a dick. Farming out her kid like that to support a habit. But it takes all kinds to fill the world. I guess.

Life for Colleen didn't start out this way, not even close to this way. Steering a two something pound Ruskie into the trunk of his own

1

car by his eyelid and wrist lock that would result in breakage with the slightest resistance was something she had come close to daydreaming on but, never close to realizing. Until these last few years. I think he could be a Soviet.

Nope, life started out depressingly average in her mind. Loving family, Dad was a bit of a prick of a zen riddle but hey, move past it. Mom, a daughter couldn't have asked for better, friends, other family, blah, blah, yada, yada. Finished high school, did a bunch of different menial tasks that her fellow schmucks call employment. Until most immediate family weren't around anymore. Then she drifted away from friends, needing the solitude more than the companionship. Before this, she never really steered her life by her own navigational guideposts.

The last two to three years of hitching, north, east, south and west, whenever and why-ever be damned. And it felt like how she should have been living her life since she was fifteen. She also was at the tipping point of only existing in corporeal form that others rarely glimpsed her. Passport, health care, bank accounts... who needs em. It was getting a bit harder to bounce into and out of neighbouring countries but, doable.

If I'm only carrying a large rucksack, and if it's not containing any real terror for anyone, who cares! Borders, there's another word of interest. Countries bureaucrats consider them important, a four-year-old with a colouring book sees them as lines on a page. Who's more astute to realities? Judging by what one hears from any voters about how the term years are going, have gone or what could be expected of the next ones, maybe the four-year-old is better suited to make decisions for their fellow citizens. Hell, then at least any mistakes would be honest ones.

I bet the snake in the trunk would run for office if he hadn't stamped 'dangerous sociopath' all over his former life choices. Despite his actions I witnessed personally, I can usually recognize one of my own kind. I just refrain, like a behavioural diet. I only behave like this when there is someone on the menu who's done too much of their own dining. Honestly, when they cross my path, it's like the cosmic forces are whispering, "Colleen, here's another creature all other creatures would be better off without. Do with as you choose, we trust your judgment. And as always with great gratitude for balancing the scales. Sincerely yours, the universe." Or something like...

"Ah, ha! There you are. You elusive little can of spray-paint!"

After placing her sack on the curb, she got to work on the windshield, "FAILED RAPIST IN TRUNK". Clear, concise and accurate. Leaving the can on the hood after the tagging work was complete. Probably chemical tests that could connect certain batches of paint to the paint on the glass, why hold onto evidence, long hair under a tuque, gloves on the whole time in the car and all clothes previously purchased second hand, thrift stores are awesome, best of luck investigators.

After the last four or five times, it occurred to Colleen that a pattern could be emerging. Leaving all these fallen angels in embarrassing circumstances for later discovery.

"YOU HEAR ME WHORE?!"

"Pffft, sore loser." Colleen muttered. Not my fault, as per usual, stick out thumb, define ride details, secure ride, exit vehicle. If I wanted more than that, I would have been clear in the beginning before even entering the car, hell, they all were even guilty of that, breaking a contractual agreement. Probably wouldn't stand up in courtroom. Colleen smirked.

Only once was she standing over a deceased in all of these disappointing encounters with fellow members of her species. If the gun hadn't been pulled on Colleen, she may have been tempted to stave in her skull with the road pylon.

Those things have a really heavy base... yes tempted but, no, I would have refrained. Another sore loser, who deprived herself of the indignity of any losses, ever again.

Maybe that was why Colleen regarded her as the worst, she chose to leave Colleen with two choices: to either die and leave that kid to future abuses, or kill the bitch. Colleen's smirk had perished at the first few firings of neurons of her remembering.

It changes you, watching the life drain out of someone's eyes, not for the better or the worse but you're never quite the same.

Colleen could snuff out another numb-crotch again, of either gender and maybe would. Not like humans are commonly known to end another's life, without actual cause and definitely not for anything material. A pure more respectable motive, like that of any creature fighting for more life, to survive. Or for more life and continued survival of others. Shouldering her pack, she started up the hill as previously decided, thinking an observation of the discovery was risky but also maybe informative. If a good hide could be located, she may catch in conversation about her other exploits and the emergence of a pattern. Or not? After months of training and a consistent sleep schedule, Colleen had not only succeeded at a mental alarm for time, but also for whatever ambient noises she may wish to be woken by.

She programmed herself, brakes squeal, tires slowing on pavement, car door opening and hard-soled comfortable shoes grinding on rocks embedded in the asphalt.

Once she was satisfied with her programming and position, Colleen smiled and then let herself drift off, nestled deep inside a large bush.

Coming to with a start and the sensation of only just moments ago having drifted off, she watched a vehicle approach. Not law enforcement but, familiar. Big, a bit flashy, a bit too flashy and looking like it was a second car of her trunk tenant.

Interesting.

Two men got out and the obviousness of it hits, organized crime, her pal in the trunk seemed to be talking less trash than she previously assessed. Impotent and screaming threats he has no hopes of carrying out is just that, limpness. However, having others, above you or under you to act when you can't, because maybe you're locked in the trunk of your own car? Could come in handy. Not against me, maybe other's. Colleen was already gaming out how the two newcomers would make for decent cargo as well. The two men talked in their native tongue, at which point my trunk-contained-big-talker yelled out. It was obvious they both recognized the voice emitting from the load compartment. "Boss?" Said the one with a hand to his mouth, poorly hiding his smile.

"GET ME THE HELL OUTTA HERE, YOU IDIOT!" The reply came, knocking humour to the curb.

Colleen watched as Idiot opened the drivers door and hit the trunk release. The two newcomers did remarkably well hiding their amusement, after their boss climbed out and stood facing them. For thirty seconds they stood facing him and no words were exchanged. Finally, Idiot, as Colleen knew him to be, broke the silence.

"We were just on our way to your place, a call came in for a contract here in town. We wanted to see how you wanted it handled."

"Humph, I gotta be honest," the boss grumped, "I could use the release of closing someone's eyes. I've had better days." The two men looked on expectantly, not wanting to ask but itching to know. "Tell me more about this termination, any reason we can't do it tonight?"

"Actually, there's a rush on it, done before midnight is the order from Salenko, this bitch must've crossed the line in some real bad way and crossed some real bad people. It was actually pressed to us to move on it if we couldn't speak with you about it inside the hour."

From her vantage angle, Colleen witnessed the smile form on her former trunk tenant's face at the news of it being a woman.

"Well then," looking at his watch, "We have four hours to get it done and report in. I can afford to enjoy things a bit, get some frustrations..." He stopped when both men were again looking expectantly, still wondering why he had been occupying his own trunk.

Colleen was rapidly calculating how she could prevent this unknown woman's demise and certain suffering.

No transport, I left the keys in the dipshit's cup holder, on foot with a pack too heavy to run with and no parked vehicles in sight. Not even a kids bike with tassels on the handlebars was showing itself as an option.

It finally looked as if Colleen's ride to this resort town was going to say something to his men in explanation to why he was locked in his own trunk when a vehicle's sounds of approach made them all turn to the front of the car. A marked police cruiser rolled up and slowed, the driver's window rolling down.

Well this is fortunate, gives me some time to find a ride. A police officer when you need one, may just be able to...

The officer nodded, "Evening, Mr. Addams." Then stopped speaking with his mouth hanging open as he read the painted message on the windshield that caught his eye. "Jeez, I'll be looking into any vandalism activity right away, I mean, if you don't mind leaving it to me, finding the punks that vandalized your car."

Oh, I don't like this at all, 'Evening Mr Addams'! Really? Colleen thought, Doesn't seem like his real name to go with that accent, and this officer regards him as someone with authority.

"Officer Stebans, no, no, this is no concern with the locals of your fair town. It's a private matter, though, you will keep eyes open for a dyke'ish girl with a large black backpack. Black tuque and clothing, not a local and someone you report location to me and then forget about seeing her."

"Uh, sure thing Mr. Addams, I'll be sure to call you if I see anyone like that. Okay, you gents have a good night."

Shit! Not only have I wasted the little time I had to find transport, now the law will be on the look out for someone matching my description... think Colleen, think!

"We'll take your car boys, mine is more conspicuous than I'd like, we'll come back and sort it out later." The three men walked back to the other car and loaded in.

With the keys still in the cup holder where I left them, the transport I require awaits me. When things roll like this, I hear the universe saying, "Go forth Colleen and balance the scales as you see fit." Perfect, they've three point turned and gone the other way, guaranteed they ain't coming back this way. A quick look up and down the street, yup, go, go, go!

She was in the car and yanking the shifter into reverse the second the motor caught. Colleen had the ignition key sliding home before her full weight had settled into the seat. Closing the door only after the car was rolling backwards. Her quarry had turned on the next street and were out of sight. Can't lose 'em! Colleen could make any vehicle cry for mercy. The next street came up fast, she never bothered to turn around and just took the corner in reverse.

No headlights for the stooges to see in the rear view, only if I braked would the taillights flash crimson on this dark night. "Hm... looks to be getting dark in the other way also." Colleen whispered to herself.

Again in her thoughts, "Maybe I am just another so-and-so and yet again I'm not, most people would have witnessed what I had, and done what? They probably wouldn't be following the bad men in one of their own cars, in reverse, in the hopes of intervening on a stranger's behalf. A stranger, who logic could suggest, may be as immoral as those coming to kill her. Even so, the idea of it being an enjoyment for that dipshit, making it hard and drawing it out for the victim. Shit, I shoulda found an empty nowhere spot and ran a garden hose from the muffler into that trunk. You just never know until you actually know, and his goons would've did the dirt-cheap deed anyway. And they may have made for more suffering for their victim as well. Colleen slowed on the uphill in neutral and let the turned front tire gently rest against the curb. Her quarry had stopped the next block up. She left it running, in case they were address hunting. Nope, they have the right place.

Colleen wouldn't make a move until she evaluated. She never did.

I could use this car to ram into them, time it right and they'll be out of it when the collision happens. Nope, thinking I'm on foot from here, gotta move.

The men all congregated by the trunk. The mass of stuff they collected from the load compartment of the car developed all sorts of dark thoughts and ideas in Colleen's mind.

Body disposal and transport materials, torture and dismemberment apparatus. Hell, the two henchmen were carrying duffles so large that just one would hold me and leave room for another half of me. These pricks have done this shit before, rolling around with readiness for dirty deeds in the trunk.

Colleen was nearing the lot where they had parked in front, when they were just at the task of gaining entry. She slowed from a run to skipping, literally, on the balls of her feet. She was twenty-five feet from their backs and they were none the wiser.

"Shit, boss, the door ain't locked, what ya figure?"

"Don't know, don't care, time for me to get my freak on, I'm gonna enjoy this," Mr A seethed as he was removing from the duffle one of the most uniquely terrifying blades Colleen had ever seen. Maybe I'll souvenir it after I use it for stirring your intestines, Mr A. After I deal with these three clowns, then I determine whether their target is any different then they are.

She was tucked in against the grill of a big Chevy Avalanche in the driveway well before the three men looked back to the street for anything of concern. She heard the orders given, one stayed out front and one went in with the boss.

Nice when your enemies divide themselves for you to conquer. And I have already decided. I'm gonna subjugate these pricks. To extremes. Oh look, a sturdy aluminum snow shovel, an excellent pacification appliance.

With three steps she was standing on a light fixture on one corner of the garage clutching the gutter. Her steps were rear bumper, tailgate and outdoor light. Approaching footsteps were her reward for the slightest deliberate drag of the shovel on the cement driveway. What work your opponent does, you don't have to. Colleen's only concern was that henchmen one would clear the corner before the fixture tore free of the wall. Ah, there it is, silencer, pistol, hand, arm and the rest, high ground wasn't necessary. But fun though, gravity do your thing! As she stepped off and released the gutter, the guy's gun arm went up between her legs and rammed her crotch at the exact time she brought the head of the shovel flat down on his head. He crumpled as though his skeletal structure vanished from inside his body. She had reached behind her for the pistol in perfect timing to keep it from clattering on cement.

It worries me sometimes how easy these heroine shenanigans come to me. No, actually it doesn't. Baffle me? Nope, call me DARK WIDOW, or ANGEL BLACK, bah, too copycattish. Marketing and branding are truly not talents of mine, whatever.

In two seconds, she was familiar with the weapon, round chambered, full mag and safety off. By the fourth second she had cleared the corner like numb-nut one should have and was speed walking the shadows up to the front door.

Colleen's concerns of entering through the open door were none. She could see her other soon to be play-things just inside the vestibule, backs to her and looking up a spiral staircase. And then a truly lovely voice called down.

"Up here guys, second door on the left! Let's get this over with quick!"

Okay, that's just bizarro, thought Colleen. Is she expecting this? Whatever, two more numb-nuts on my agenda then weird lady upstairs. She probably has a lot of cats.

"Oh, it ain't gonna be quick bitch," Colleen heard Mr A whisper.

"It might be for your undoing," Colleen replied under her breath, "Bitch."

As the two men progressed up the stairs, a tidy arrangement of broom and broomstick dustpan came into Colleen's view. Keeping her finger out of the trigger guard Colleen tucked the gun in her waist band and had both handles clutched low, raised above her head and stabbed through the railing of the stairs before they had made it to the first landing. One handle in front of Mr A's shins and the other in behind his goon's ankles. It went badly for them both. Too close together, one carrying a heavy duffle, the other something pointy and sharp. Also the fact that they carried these things in the hands they would've used to grab the banister was of great detriment and comical result. Falling forward would've been in their favour but that blade he held out before him had Mr A lurching back to avoid that direction. His loyal lackey at his back, too close to his back and carrying a heavy bag went to step back and found broom handle behind his ankles. His only thing in reach with his free hand was his bosses left shoulder.

They made some noise in their stair tumble, dance, embrace and hug but it wasn't that loud. Idiot was dead on arrival at the bottom, Colleen seen the back of his neck collide with the banister cap and his chest was the perfect backstop for the hilt of the knife Mr A still clutched, blade disappeared deep in his own chest. Must've cleaved his heart nearly in two. He had 2-3 seconds of life for both glimpse, recognition and a last word. Looking up at Colleen's smiling face and her little finger tap of a wave. "Bitch..." he managed before his eyes glazed lifeless. Taking in the two bodies intertwined like non-missionaries in that position, Colleen knew it for a fact, no crime scene personnel on the planet could photo that without breaking out in laughter. Well, maybe not.

Better safe than sorry, she returned the janitorial equipment to their proper place put pistol in hand and scampered back out to shovel-head. He was still out for the count. Breathing but out. Now what about cat lady? All was quiet and Colleen had nothing to do anyway. Secure hotel accommodations for the night and roll out in the morn. Oh well, why not, let's see how many meow'ers she has.Back in the house, again better safe than sorry, she kept the pistol in hand and progressed up the stairs. Actually looking for tripping hazards besides the pile of meat in front of the steps. Stairs can be dangerous after all. Apparently, two in three home invaders can suffer a lethal fall on them.

Second door on the left, she cleared the first half of the room as she swung in low, the last half never more exposed than the parts of her necessary and the gun. The dame on the bed was exquisite, silk chemise house coat that opened in the front like a robe, loosely tied and... damn.

"Oh, hello, my, my, aren't you a cute little assassin. I was definitely not expecting a woman, um, maybe we could drag this out and you could, oh hell, I'm sorry. I've had a bit too much to drink. Liquid courage you could say, I just wanted to die with some dignity, maybe some grace." She finished while fingering the top of her silk robe.

Quickly regaining her composure, Colleen stopped staring, hopefully before this bombshell noticed she was doing just that. She did a quick check of the adjoining bathroom and then tried to explain.

"Slow your roll lady, I ain't here to kill ya. Just got wind of that being the scene to unfold and decided to keep that from being the case."

"Oh no! No, no, no! I wish you wouldn't have gotten involved! You can't stop this, no one can! My death is as certain as the change of seasons, practically that universal constant, maybe you can still get clear of this, if you just leave now, maybe you'll be alright!"

Colleen was stunned, what the hell was this dame into? Did she piss off the league of justice? Make enemies with plato nato? Step on one of the revengers toes? And where the hell are all her cats?

"Look, stay here, lay there waiting for the next hit team, I'm not telling you to live on or roll over but I am out of here.. Sorry for your troubles, whatever they may be and maybe we'll see you in the next life." Colleen turned for the door when she seen it in her peripherals. This gorgeous lady seemed to fall apart like Jenga with the wrong piece pulled. No, no, don't, no, don't start, dammit. She's crying, I'm useless with these emotional points in people's lives, maybe that's where I'm truly the most sociopathic. I slump against the door frame and listen to her sob.

Twenty seconds later and I'm not joking about it, if she's got cats and one gets in arm's reach of me I'm going grabby-tabby to toss one at her for drying her eyes or blowing her nose and I'm... oh for crying out loud... I grab a chair by one of those fancy tables where beauties like Aphrodite here gussy themselves up and slump into it.

Maybe I'm still a bit caring? I can't bring myself to leave her this way. "Hey, uh, lady? Look, I'm no good with this stuff, do you want to, oh, for pete's sakes." The last bit muttered under her breath and followed with the hope of it being enough under her breath to have gone unheard.

"Sniff, sob" She dried her face a bit with one sleeve. "I'm sorry, like I said, had just enough to drink to be apathetic to it all and with me that's on a tipping point of turning into an emotional bomb. Hey, thanks for not just walking out. I still think you should, and I have some measure of experience here. Literally, it's like your probability of dying raises one percent per second you're still in close proximity to me."

Geez, she has made enemies with a huge organization or Norse gods or some omnipotent forces. Maybe I have been sent on my curtain's mission, no more scale balancing for you, Colleen. Not even knowing where it came from, I bark at her, "Get dressed, pants, shirt, jacket and footwear should all be dark colours, athletic or maybe even tactical if that's available." She looked at me somewhat dumbfounded and then gave a quick nod and got to it.

The glance into her robe as she walked past me was a gift worthy for Venus. I'm seeing a perfect still of her inner right thigh as it became a sculpture of abdominal perfection and the glimpse of a side profile of breast at the end of that lower torso road. OH GODESSES, I AM NOT WORTHY. If a second hit team walked in now catching me totally off guard and all life up to this moment was shit, it would have been a more than excellent last view.

Colleen was impressed, the woman was ready in four minutes, dark clothing, acceptable footwear and a small backpack shouldered and ready. "You have any cash, or valuables untraceable?"

"It's in the bag" she indicated with a glance over her shoulder, "Also, no phone or any technology is packed, it's all left behind. I have more cash in a safety deposit box here in town."

Impressive, Colleen thought. "Have a good full roll of tinfoil in the kitchen?"

"Uh, ya, follow me."

"First, grab your phone, just never know if having a traceable item may be what a situation requires." The bombshell smiled and showed comprehension in her eyes. Grabbed a phone off the table by the door and led the way out. Following her, Colleen was both impressed and relieved, impressed that she seemed to have turned to a, "Screw it, let's roll with the punches," stance on things and relieved because finding a eye drying or nose blowing calico was no longer a top priority.

They finished up in the kitchen in less than 30 seconds and she went to lead them out the door when Colleen grabbed her arm, turning her about face. She had a momentary look of terror at which point Colleen realized she still held the gun with silencer somewhat aimed at her. Colleen also realized her whole appearance and demeanour was that of someone who could walk into a lady's bedroom and triple-tap her before turning to walk out. Colleen was always quick to switch into lethal operator mode. A coral snake, calmly floating beneath the surface, amidst the oceans currents. "Sorry," she said, changing the gun's trajectory, "But from here on out, I take point, okay?"

It took a few seconds for the terror expression to shift to doubt, then a few more to shift to embarrassment. "I'm sorry," she replied. "For a second there I thought you were gonna kill me and all this was just some sadistic game play, I'm so embarrassed."

Colleen smirked, then replied, "One way you know that to be the case is, you'd be armed and in all ways conveying the intent to kill me. Other than that, you have nothing to worry about. Talk me through it, this go into the garage?"

"Yes, light switch is right of the door."

Excellent Colleen thought as she squeezed all four tires. Hanging up on a wall-mount-rack, nicely out of the way were two mountain bikes. One hard tail and one soft tail and decent mountain bikes at that.

"Is now the best time for some cardio and training of your bum, I mean sure you could afford to tone up a little but.."

Colleen turned to see a playful expression and could only think of one response, regretting it as the last word slipped off her tongue, "Bite my ass."

"Promises, promises," she said, with appetite in her eyes and a provocative bite on her bottom lip.

Colleen turned away to hide the tells she was sure her own face was advertising as blatant as half the neon glow of Vegas. If I had money to take, this Aphrodite could ruin me and I'd thank her from the gutter. As Colleen lifted the first bike down, she replied, "Don't all you townies take bike rides for health? We should blend right in."

Which was when she remembered she needed to be more 'blendy' than she was. Officer Stebans was still out there on lookout for Colleen in her current garb. "Any bike trails we could get lost on that will lead us out to a scungy motel?"

"You mean bike trails us townies would use and a hotel we would look down on?" She replied playfully "Yeah I have gated access in the back yard to the paths and if we go left, grab the first right and keep right at all forks it will take us right to gasoline alley, the hotel for un-townie like folk is right in behind the big rig gas station."

I'm more impressed with, shit, I don't even know her name. With my back turned to her as I reach up for the second bike I show my usual swan-on-fire grace around pretty women. "Colleen" I say, somewhat embarrassed "That's me, I mean, shit" I hear stifled laughter behind me and hang my head. Only to have it snap to attention at the sharp and surprisingly painful pinch on my left butt cheek, feeling a slight amount of pressure where the thumb knuckle was actually ringing my backdoor like a push bell. The pinch didn't abate and actually got more severe when I feel and hear the growl in my ear.

"Not to worry, first-time introductions can be awkward, you'll try again later and maybe do a better job, maybe even adequate enough to earn my name, Colleen!" She said my name with a sneer and finished with a gentle nibble on my earlobe. Then without dialing back on the pinch, yanked her hand away. I swore my butt cheek was still flapping when we both rolled our bikes into the backyard. I knew for certain this lady could own me, feeling the dampness in my skivvies when I mounted the bike seat.

2

Colleen had brought them to a stop on a hill with a decent vantage point of the hotel and neighbouring fuel station. And the perspective was good enough to to see a police cruiser parked out front of a greasy eats with window view of the hotel office. Shit, my monocular is in my duffle back in that bush. "Surveillance?" Her unnamed beauty asked, to which Colleen replied with a nod and pointing to the police car. "The guy on top, at the bottom of your stairs, I kinda upset him earlier on by throwing him in his own trunk."

"Oh! Wow! You are a feisty little thing, aren't cha! And what about those guys entwined like that on my floor? They looked quite close."

Colleen smiled into the black. Then heard Beautiful ask.

"So are we concerned about the police so soon?"

"Well, if it's the same cop that rolled up when I was surveilling, on-top guy gave him my description and orders to be looking for me. Just wish I had my monocular for a better look."

"Oh, here, you can use my optics, little miss unprepared," she said playfully, while she unshouldered her backpack which was mated with a playfully subtle shoulder check, which also could have been accidental. And not playful or intentional.

I'm about as good as an amoeba at reading courtship signals. "You're worse than that, I would say." You hush and leave me alone with this gorgeous crush.

Colleen's inner mind shenanigans continued as she looked through the proffered binoculars. Nice quality field glasses. Colleen recognized the officer in the diner, looking out the window, "Yup, that's Barney Fife, probably deduced I would need a hotel room, being from outta town."

"So what do we do? Call in an accident, set a fire somewhere?"

"Nope, I'm just gonna stroll into the diner and chat with him," replied Colleen.

After they had secured their room and took their bikes in, Colleen explained she would be right back and walked out. Heading directly towards the diner. She seen that officer Stebans recognized her as a possible for the description he was given before she pushed in the door. Knowing he had eyes on her because she was looking right at him all the way from the room she just left.

Never having slowed, Colleen walked right up and slid in to a seat opposite of Stebans just before he said "Ma'am," half questioningly and half ordinary greeting.

Colleen raised a wait a sec finger and the waitress arrived with the customary question "Coffee?"

Colleen was halfway through righting a cup and sliding it over, then in a British accent said, "Thanks love." Which brought an instant blush to her plump and quite adorable face.

"Menu?"

"No dear, may have something to go over at the hotel later tonight though."

The waitress nodded and smiled while turning back for the kitchen.

Officer Stebans looked nervous, and repeated the half greeting, half question, "Ma'am?"

Colleen smiled, having already studied her table company and made her plan for the rather one-sided conversation that would take place. She carried on with the accent, confusing things can be a go

The Mt-Saint-Helen's-of response came out of Colleen before she knew it. "Hey, you beautiful bitch! You could respect me enough to look at me and hear me out!"

Her hand dropped from the handle and she stayed still as rock. Colleen was starting to sweat, tremble and thought she may even put old Saint Helen's to shame, but with an explosion of pure embarrassment.

Then slowly, she turned to face Colleen and with effort it appeared, keeping a deadpan face when she spoke, "You're right, well go on then."

"I'm not too good at it, interaction, and that's when there isn't anything really there. Then with you, you're so damn, like knock out, bombshell... so," she didn't so much interrupt as see the stall in my explanation.

With a swift reposition of her hands on her hips, taking a step closer to me ending up at arms reach. Then she adopted this authoritative and domineering persona. "Continue!" she barked.

"And then you come on full dominatrix minus the garb, I mean wow. If you ever needed a fallback career, you've got one! So I'm just needing to tell you, you haven't misread anything, and me not joining you last night, let alone full tilt running over and diving right in, I may actually now have a life regret that is, damn. I'm also not the most attractive thing around and I know it, but with you I feel unworthy in that and numerous other regards to even kneel in front of you! There, I guess that's it, uh, thanks, thanks for listening."

I averted my eyes, slapped my knees, moving to rise, saying, "Okay, now we..." When her hand stopped my upward motion, palm pressing firmly on my forehead. Fingers slightly moving through my hair like a delicate insect, with goose bumps developing, I looked up to see her face, the smile more in her eyes than on her lips. With darkness there, she pulled her hand back and stopped, closed three fingers and thumb, the index remaining out pointing, the universal down gesture. I shivered. Slipping out of the chair in compliance, I knelt before her. She kept that darkness in her face with a predatory grin and moved her hand to cup under my chin. Firmly, but sensually, she held my chin, tilting my face up more. "Maybe, maybe you'll still prove yourself worthy of my name." Then, she moved her hand up, she ruffled my hair and sneered, "Colleen!"

Turning about face, saying playfully and cheerful as ever, "Okay, we can go now." Calling out when she reached the door and grasped its handle, "Heel! You beautiful bitch!" She opened the door and walked out into the sunshine.

I knelt there for a few beats utterly dumbfounded. "I'm gonna kill her," I muttered as I realized I was heading to the door walking on kneecaps for the first few knee steps.

3

They sat in a coffee shop, across from the bank and talked it over. In, out and gone. My nameless crush seemed nervous. "Look, we could just leave it for now and blow town. There is some risk in the plan. But we're not past the PSR here."

"PSR?" She asked.

"Point of Safe Return, when you've used up more than half of whatever, might as well just keep plowing forward because going back is no longer an option," I explained.

"Were you military? Because you seem to have an interesting grasp of things, from which one could infer you have a background to match."

Colleen looked at her nameless crush, who neither blinked or looked away for some time. "You knew what the acronym meant." I said with some accusation, yet smiling.

Watching her as she grabbed her iced whatever the heck it was, her lips opened over the straw, then she said while poorly hiding the smirk, "Maybe."

I smirked while looking away out the window, still seeing nothing of concern. "Well, maybe, I can deduce that you have some background of your own. As for me, and this is utterly true, I've indulged in too many movies and switched to books. Now I may be on the 'too many' front with those as well. I've also studied a lot of combat, tactical awareness and battle strategy."

She looked back at Colleen seemingly more interested then before, "I gather that you gathered I'm nervous, in truth I am nervous but more so about not having this again than anything else bad that could happen."

"This?" I asked.

She rolled her eyes and replied while she made a wave that included, her, I and the establishment, "This you dumb-ass, us sitting here, chatting and interacting. Like it's more I was angry about the missed opportunity last night than the thought of being rejected. You and I in a coffee shop, or us in a scuzzy motel, as things are, they may be opportunities we have only this one time and not again."

I thought for a second and then said, "You're right, and you nailed it down, what I tried to convey about that regret of mine. Let's say we have another night in another scuzzy motel. Or another morning in some coffee spot. Or another twenty of both. We still won't have number 21 because I didn't make the most of it."

They both sat for a time not saying anything, just looking at each other. It was nice, not awkward and uncomfortable, but simply nice.

A thought occurred to Colleen and she was surprised about it herself. But spat it out anyway. "I have a notion, when circumstances allow it, we take these times by the clit and make sure to smell the roses.

Here we are, possible moments from demise but we have these moments. So when we can, we do. Your thoughts?"

"A quickie in the bathroom probably isn't what you're suggesting, I take it." She said with a smirk. "But I like the notion, so... how's about three questions and three answers a piece, no pressure of judgment, just honesty and hopefully some smiles and laughs?"

"You're awesome, you know that," Colleen said, "and never let anyone tell you different." Which got Colleen her first blush from her nameless crush. "So, you first?"

"No, technically that was your first and kind of a wasted question if you ask me."

Colleen looked down and slapped her forehead, then shook her head, then looked up grinning, gave a mock bow and waited.

"Are you a sociopath?"

Screw it, Colleen thought, honesty and no pressure of judgment here we go. "Yes. I would have to say yes." Before continuing, with their eyes locked, Colleen was shocked at those beautiful eyes looking back, with no discernible judgment. "I always try to keep it animal-like," getting an eyebrow raise and whimsical smile for that. "It's like an older more primitive form of us knew it to be wrong but with certain scenarios like protection and base survival we flicked that switch to, "I don't care mode," to see another day, to see to it that ours and theirs see another as well."

Colleen let that simmer for a while and then said "Look, this may be going too far but..."

A raised hand, "No pressure, no judgment, only honesty, just ask," she reassured Colleen.

"Okay," Colleen started again, opened her mouth, nothing, a moment more hesitation and then she blurted it out. "What's your favourite colour?"

Her response mimicked my earlier forehead slap and shaking lowered her head with a smile of her own. "Alright, you want to waste a question joking around, thats fine. Okay, little miss two questions down, my turn."

Colleen shook her head, "Nope, uh-uh, I'm not playing anymore. I asked and you're not being honest with me." Colleen could barely keep her roar of laughter bottled up. She looked out the window trying for a facial expression of pouting.

Now it was Colleen's nameless crush that opened her mouth, hesitated, then fired out the words. "It's stupid, or at least I think it is but, well I hate the coldest days of winter but I love winter for its absence of most colours. It's like all plant life on earth, geology, even bodies of water, they wage war with their respective colours. Then that first snowfall, it whites out everything bringing peace to it all. My favourite would technically be black or white, either all of them in unity or none at all. But I guess it's white, like the first heavy snowfall. Its stupid, I know."

I looked at her for several seconds, just hoping that some day she could see me the way I was seeing her now and that was the way she seen that first snowfall. Pure, peaceful, beauty.

"What?" she asked.

Which yanked me out of a daze, "Oh, sorry, I was thinking of that chaos of colours that rages on in all of us. That was astoundingly insightful. No, not stupid at all."

Now she looked at me, maybe even in the way I had been looking at her. "So we're down to my two left and your one remaining."

"No, you have one left, same as me."

"No cheating, Colleen, or else there will be consequences. I have two questions left to your one."

"No, when I was dazed and amazed with your colour answer, you asked me, "what?" like what was I thinking. I just assumed you went for your next question there and then, so I told you honestly my answer."

She glared at Colleen, then smiled and said, "Touché, so it is, and this is me stating a fact, if ever I am to be your full-on dominatrix, I'll do all that's necessary to exert extreme domination, and you know you do all things necessary to deserve it."

"Promises, promises," Colleen replied. "And now I'm actually thinking I'd like to ask my question a little later. Really give myself something to live for and fight tooth and nail to see my next day. A day where both of us are across from each other at some establishment."

"I'm in total agreement, we will reconvene at a later time and another venue."

Then, they both just sat there, staring into each others eyes, smiling the minutes away.

The whole bank experience took 15 minutes, she knew, having watched the clock. Every minute seemed to drag out longer than was fair, it was time away from that adorably frumpy little action hero she felt so into. Even in the event of agonizing death, her regret was to not be able to see Colleen again, across a table in some other establishment. Shit, not giving her my name. Dying would be nothing compared to the tragedy of not looking her in the eyes when I tell Colleen my name. I'm gonna live, if only just for that one experience.

She was in the secondary entrance with the ATMs, hand on the outer most door, pushed it open two inches and waited. The sound of the big block v-8 at full revs was how Colleen described it, an end of the world roar, and it meant she had to be ready, no hesitation. She heard the squeal of tires and seconds later the Blazer was rocking on its shocks on the sidewalk. She slid out the door and leapt up through the other that Colleen popped opened for her. Then was slammed into the seat with the full force of the motor in the K5 Blazer as Colleen turned the wheel to the street.

Colleen liked standards, any performance issues with shifting were on the operator of the vehicle, with an automatic, it shifted and changed RPM's without the operator's consent. There's a lot of reasons NASCAR's aren't automatics. As she power-shifted into third gear, a quick glance in the rear views told her the teams weren't mobile yet. They were good, she only just spotted them when her crush was just into the secondary entrance. But they weren't ready with their vehicles, the grab van was in place but the other car should have had a driver at the wheel like the van. Good coordination can buy you seconds.

After the last corner she took, it looked to be all clear to take her planned route. Too bad, gonna miss this rig. The road she was on wound up the hill, paralleling a high-end housing part of town, with a treeline to her left.

It looked like a dead end which she knew it would be for their pursuing parties. The van they had was two-wheel drive with not much ground clearance; their car was worse off yet. And the road deactivation she was about to navigate would hang up the k-5 if it was incorrectly executed. "Hang on gorgeous! This is gonna be a bit rough!" Colleen hollered with glee. She had the rig in four high since the beginning of the bank escape so in first it was gonna be a bit faster than the owner may want to take this truck down the dip and back up the other side. At the bottom her angle was perfect, light bumper scrape on front and the rear nothing at all and the truck suspension's articulation was enough that the momentum loss was minimal.

Coming up the other slope that was about the length of the truck and at least a forty-five degree incline felt like the climb you take on a roller coaster before the first plunge. All the weight of your body on your back into the seat. When the front tires crested they stayed on the forty-five degree trajectory as if the slope was still there but invisible.

"WEW HOO!" screamed her passenger in absolute glee.

And Colleen threw in a, "YA BABY!" of her own as the Blazer's rear tires found the end of the hill. The truck wheelied for fifteen feet, as the front end started dropping, Colleen power shifted into 2nd and kept it from slamming down real hard. When it did bounce down Colleen again glanced to the rear view and seen the two cars halt just before the pavement ended, both passengers leapt out and reached for weapons. "HEADS DOWN!" Colleen cried out. They both ducked low right before the rear window blew out, other shots sounding off the body like maniacs were beating the steel with ball peen hammers.

Colleen was a bit hesitant to show some of her real self until her passenger cried out again, a loud, "HA HA! YOU ASSHATS CAN'T STOP THESE BITCHES!"

"OH YA!" Matched Colleen as she turned the truck hard into the next corner, and then cranking the steering all the way opposite for the over-steer into the drifting of the rear end.

They were doing 40km/h with no concerns reaching the stopping point a minute later. She had scouted the route out on pedal bike this morning by moonlight, having found the spot where locals walked through to get where they were headed. Lots of foot traffic prints and the road went straight for some time. "Ready?" I asked my beauty queen of a passenger. Yeah, my Queen is who she is to me. It'll work until I actually get her name. She nodded in reply, smiling. Gosh, I appreciate that smile. Colleen slowed to a safe speed and set the cruise, looked for the dead tree on the left and started the count. She had already tied off the steering wheel. They literally stepped out into a run as the truck growled off down the road. As if it were happy to help aid in their plan.

A few minutes later and they were on boards wearing all the expected gear including hill passes for the day, carving down the slope like they'd been doing it all morning. When they hit the bottom, they went in and mingled, having found a group of Swedes that were rolling out and had room for them and all their gear inside of ten minutes. From bank break to careening down the highway out of town had taken less than twenty-three minutes.

It was more a stroke of luck with the Swedes than they had hoped for, they were done financially with their vacation and were going to press hard for the next city with a major airport. Turn in their rental van and fly home, which meant a respectable four hours from where the most heat was on. Colleen figured they were safe for a day or two, especially if they changed it up with their appearance. Which was easy for Colleen, she had on a Harley Davidson bandana and had done some glue on facial hair from a basic costume and disguise kit she always hauled in her duffle. The Swedes had laughed when Colleen had dug her rucksack out of a snow bank in the parking lot of the ski hill but seemed more impressed with the methodology than curious about why.

It was just nearing dinner time when they had secured lodgings and got into their room. The awkwardness started two minutes later when they both tried expressing the same sentiment, just not word for word. Their words gave the audible visual of a train wreck, IKEA furniture, processed field grains and Beanie Babies strewn all over heck's half acre.

"Would you mind..

"Would it be okay...

Then it went weird again with the whole, no, no, you go first and then they both started laughing. They ended up with hands on each others shoulders like a pre-teen dance in elementary school before we learn the waist and hand position. And they kept on laughing to the point of glistening eyes.

It was mutual, they both wanted an hour or so to themselves and wanted to meet for drinks in the adjoining lounge later. Colleen said that they had to do some quick wig and jewellery work though. So ten minutes in their bathroom with Colleen's disguise kit and her crush looked like a different person. Hair style, much more aggressive, make up styling, easily dominatrix suitable. Then some fake piercings for the nose and top of ear and even some dental add on's that would throw facial recognition a curve ball it couldn't hit.

But it didn't stop there, she insisted on doing up some make up for Colleen. Which was not contested by Colleen, first, a little more confusion is always a good thing and second, Colleen was certain she was in good hands. Her crush had been wearing make up that first night and it looked like professional work done for a movie star. While she worked, she also explained.

"You see, with foundation and skin tones, you accentuate on a person's strengths. This is flattery, not insult, you have some tough and mean to your facial structure, bone position and depth. So you do more to draw out a bit of this and a bit of that and... Voila!" As she had said that cheesy magic word and turned me to face the mirror, my jaw dropped. And this drew a giggle from my crush, and then another firm but sensual grip under my chin, pushing my jaw closed. "You don't need to be all mouth agape Colleen, unless I'm sitting on your face!"

Again with that sexy sneer in her tone when she used my name. And the reference to the domineering physical activity had me feeling heat within my netherworld. A hug felt cheesy but, some kind of embrace seemed warranted. In the mirror, our reflections were looking into our counterpart's eyes and it seemed perfect to just lean into her, my head just resting under her jaw. As it also seemed perfect when I knew what I wanted to say, "Thank you, Mistress."

She brought her arms around me, a hug from behind, "Oh my slave sweetie, you're so welcome, so very welcome."

I brought my hands up, to find hers, our fingers intertwined and we just stood there in that spooning embrace, eyes locked on each others. Many thanks to all those who contributed to the conception of mirrors.

They both parted ways with two separate cabs out in front of the hotel and ten minutes later Colleen was again struggling. As usual, it was with what most women may find simple. Buying a dress.

"I want to look beautiful for someone, her favourite colour is the pure white of a freshly fallen snow and I want it to be perfect." said Colleen somewhat matter of fact like, but also somewhat drill sergeant to a subordinate. Only it was said to a nice little older lady at the dress shop the cabbie suggested. She looked slightly bemused and then replied.

"We like a customer that knows what she wants, makes our lives easier, let me tell you dear. Right this way my decisive lovely. I have several cuts of dress that meet the majestic white of pure snow, is this a formal type event, wedding or proper affair?"

Colleen liked her very much, she didn't know if it was procedure but she was leaving this cool little bird a tip. "It's just meeting for drinks but I still feel it's a special night, so sexy but not too... improper?"

"We are women, we can be proper in a bordello wearing burlap. And I won't rest here tonight until you're confident of you being dressed so as to impress. With it being drinks, it opens up our possibilities. Seeing your form, hear me now dear, you have hips that slender women hate when they stand beside you, you both wearing similar dresses, mid thigh in length, I think. You'll make it look good."

That feisty little dress shop lady was all sorts of correct, though Colleen had never tried to, she looked in the mirror and felt it. "I look good!" When she came back around with the heels, she carried a hand bag that looked like you'd lose it if it fell in the snow.

"Now dear, I know you cringed a tad at the prices so I just want you to have this, it's something I do once a year with those special customers. It's not a recent model of bag and it really isn't that expensive but..."

Colleen interrupted her with a hug she hoped wasn't too out of line and then on exit of the embrace said, "I'll take it on trade for you being honest with me on what a most awesome guide through these foreign lands of fabrics should be getting for gratuity.

The little soul's eyes glistened as she said, "There isn't a usual gratuity." Colleen threw down twenty percent without a second thought. As she rode back to the hotel in the cab that her dress shop friend had called for her, she thought, screw it. Her nameless crush had given her a wad of cash so that they both had a few eggs in more than one basket. Besides, Colleen had spent most of her own money anyway, she would've been shy the cost of the heels she wore and the tip she left. Colleen had contemplated buying a wig, and ended up doing so. Just for the hopes of some fun at her Queen's expense.

***

She sat at a table off to the side of the bar, stirring her drink, looking at the clock and feeling insecure. I gave her some cash and she bolted, right! I thought we had something and then the crush of reality, I'm gonna get wasted if she never shows. Maybe she's back at the room, all nervous and self conscious? As she glanced at the bar, a nice looking form in the most whitest of dresses, she had ever seen was subtly but not too subtly looking her way. She's got to be doing well. If she's an escort, I'd pay out heavily for that kind of dream, to be made into reality. She looked away, back at the clock and drummed her fingers on the table impatiently.

Colleen could hardly contain herself. We had looked right at each other and my crush, who will give me her damn name tonight, didn't even recognize me! After getting her drink, she stood and focused on not screwing up the walk. Heel, toe, heel, toe, don't muck this up Colleen.

In her peripheral she noticed the escort, if that's what she was, walking over. She put on her, 'I'm flattered but waiting for someone face,' and waited for her to reach her table. Damn, she is hot.

Colleen went with the French accent, "I'm in the mood for some company and we both seem to be waiting..." she gracefully sat, then let it hang out there for her soon-to-be-named crush to say?

"I suppose that would be okay, I am waiting for someone but, at the moment I'm frustrated enough to have you sitting at my table when she finally shows. I suppose that's cruel of me."

I grinned looking off to the side while turning my drink clockwise an hour then counter an hour. "Well, yes, yes it could be a bit cruel of you, but some of us like that in a woman." In my peripheral, I caught a slight twitch in my Queen's body language. I didn't want her recognizing me until I said the words, "My name is Colleen, and you are?" Right as I turned to look directly at my Beautiful Mistress, putting elbows on table and hands under chin. The pose with the cute face I had practiced in the mirror at the dress shop.

She was about to politely excuse herself to go back to the room and stopped in shock at the name. No way, there is no way. Slowly she turned and now it was her turn to be mouth agape.

Which was when Colleen reached over, sensually cupping under her chin, pushing up gently and saying, "Now, now, that's my mouth's job, not yours, Mistress...?"

"Now I'm feeling like I'm not worthy of kneeling in front of you, if you, you are really you. I mean, damn, what did we do today that had us both screaming in glee?

Colleen felt a pang in her chest, the good kind. Her preference would always be her who is the one kneeling, or most always. She wanted to look her best for this beautiful woman. Was Colleen honest, which was almost always the case, she took devilish pleasure feeling her nameless Queen's shock, total surprise and even doubt. That she was looking to test this 'maybe Colleen' sitting before her was a cherry to top all others. "That was a unicorn," she paused, waiting to see if she'd flinch. She did, as well as her face read enough concern that Colleen decided to be kind. Reign her usual jerk'ish self in. She dropped the accent and alliterated, "It was a unicorn because of all its uniqueness, a k-5 with the Hurst stick shift, air conditioning and factory lockers with a block change to a 454, then we boarded once down a slope to a chalet, met some Swedes, and I want us to embrace in front of our hotel mirror again the way we did before, with me looking like this."

Seeing the wave of relief on her face, made Colleen think, shit, a twenty something percent gratuity, I'd like to buy that little dress shop lady a house, or her dream luxury car. I smiled, with glee.

"You clean up real nice, my little subby." With all the affection she could muster into the statement, her facial expression and body language communicated far more than words. Reaching her hand across, meeting Colleen's, they intertwined fingers and held hands for a long time just looking into each other.

4

Sellkritch, was not a patient man and to say that he was on edge would be a monolithic understatement. It was nearing the twenty-four-hour time frame. In all my past experiences and they were many, that was bad. Unravel time and when the mayhem starts, people die. Usually the case, but this far along, people unintended. He'd, ordered it, overseen it and done the killing himself. Even in...

"KNOCK, KNOCK," at his expensive mahogany double doors broke his thoughts.

"Enter!" he bellowed, with a touch more rage than he wanted to unleash.

The man he considered capable to take over for him one day opened both doors and stepped through. The doors closed automatically. Sellkritch wanted the doors shut but soon realized the norm was people turned their back on him to close them. He didn't like being in a room with someone's back to him. Could care less about the whole respect aspect, no, it was about the eyes. You can't read a man's shoulder blades. What the fuck they gonna say, we are in a jacket right now?

The man quickly yet with great control travelled the thirty feet of office floor to end up five feet in front of the Conan Doyle replica desk without uttering a word. That was about the respect.

"Anything to report?"

"No sir, no new information. We had our report from the team still in her resort town and there was nothing to add. The dead men in the residence, the activity at the bank, the chase up into the hills and then the abandoned blazer. Then sighted at the chalet, I like that bit."

The way Sellkritch felt right now, he didn't want to admit liking money, but he respected the man's opinion. He used his self-control over his physical as a bridge to reign in his emotions. Selkritch shifted less than prey would notice, he the predator, a waiting stillness... His twenty-five-year-old chair stayed silent.

"Ya, I like that bit as well. That was insightful of you to surmise the chalet before going on a fruitless search of the woods."

"Thank you sir."

"Explain it to me."

"They must have stashed equipment somewhere for going down the slope to..."

Sellkritch didn't let him finish. "No, I got all that. What had you think chalet over a fruitless search of the woods?"

"I board sir."

"Board?"

"Snowboard, I should have said. Not for a while but when I can, I do. So I had the idea myself, it being an effective method to attain a large lead on my pursuers if I was being hunted. From that point to the chalet on skis or a board would take a three to five minutes depending on rate of carving. To walk it, twenty to twenty five minutes and the shortest route by car was thirteen minutes according to navigation."

Very smart, Sellkritch thought. He has his own experience, his own wisdom as well as conventional. Throws that all in with the new and blends it. Like he does with those disgusting looking smoothies he's always making all damn day.

"I thank you for going out there to the resort town to handle it personally." You either thank someone or you don't, putting 'I'd like to'in front of it is just bullshit, seasoned with some more excrement and served with a side order of dung.

"I know what it means to you sir, that we find the girl and sort it out before everything goes bad. I'm only here to report, I'll be leaving to go back to the airport where the trail went cold, unless you have other thoughts?"

Definitely a worthy second in command.

"The team at the girl's house, two dead and the other?"

"Still comatose, no change and one of our doctors reports it unlikely he comes out of it in a timely manner. Not timely enough to benefit our pursuit. If he had anything pertinent to say."

"You don't believe he would?"

"It looks like the point of impact to his head came from directly above, according to our physician. I would speculate he never saw the attack coming. We may get more from our team, but I'm not betting on it. All forensics were passed on to the next major department. We don't have a contact under our thumbs there."

Yet, Sellkritch thought. "I'm authorizing you to make any field decisions you feel necessary, I want this done. Locate the girl. Report by phone on the hour. Starting from when you pass the gates."

"That's how I'll do it sir. Anything else?"

"How many men with you?"

"It'll leave us thin here but I'm taking twelve. Three to a car and four cars. Each will head out in different directions from the airport approximately fifty miles. Then we wait."

Sanderdun, Sands as he went by and preferred, was right on track as far as Sellkritch was concerned. The girl wasn't hiding at the airport in a trash can. She moved on and the trail would either warm again or stay cold. Sands had a good strategy, no matter what direction she ran in, two teams may be able to converge on the hunt diagonally. One would have to back track and only leading out fifty miles would mean an hour or less behind with risky driving.

"Sir?"

Sellkritch had gotten lost in his thoughts, which only ever happened when things were personal.

"Something else, Sands?"

"Sir, I know how important this is for you. I want to hit the road in five."

"Good. Sands, we are under the gun on this already, time is not on our side, you call when you leave the property.

Sands gave a nod, turned and walked out. Sellkritch once overheard when Sands was talking with some subordinates. The gist was why say more when enough has been said. It's doing time, pointless seconds of meaningless blather when a nod would do. Sellkritch had been surprised Sands even expressed sentiment on how important this is for him. He would hate to lose a man of his qualities in something like this current fiasco, but Sands would see it as their karma. Those who kill, can meet that same end.

Sands didn't like his full name because it was his father's. Was, before Sands took it away from him. Via two in the chest and one between the eyes. More than that, he did it before his eighth birthday with his father's gun. It was the first time Sands witnessed his father wailing on his mother, at seven and a half the boy decided who wouldn't be in attendance for his next birthday. He may have been that cold natural killer before leaving his mother's protective womb.

Sellkritch stopped thinking of these events. On to the pressing present and personal score. Decades of building it all up, it was over a half century since he and twelve other boys came over in that ship. Building on a past similar to that of his second in command, he and the other twelve planned for a future. Made killers by their own volition before they knew what it meant to be men. That's why they never arrived at his age driving taxis or working construction. The remaining twelve that made up the empire, owned taxi companies, and large construction businesses.

Honest truth is those and other companies were mostly about bodies in trunks and graves unknown under buildings. Then the cell on his desk rang. He picked it up, hearing Sands on the line four minutes after he left the office.

"One hour from now sir."

"Good," Sellkritch said and hung up.

Knowing him, it'll be 59 minutes from now. For which Sands had his gratitude. It's going to be a long 59 minutes, being I'm dealing with blood and debt. He closed his eyes and his old friend creaked as he leaned all the way back, knowing he would settle this debt, no matter how many rivers the blood made. "I'll buy a fucking canoe." He muttered to the man no longer living, "My debt to you isn't paid even when I find her. Then it'll be long and I'm sure arduous, but I'll pay that debt."

He allowed himself some more thoughts as he drifted to the bloodshed before, being shed right now and the blood damn sure to be shed in times to come.

5

After 20 minutes Colleen was about to speak, breaking the silence when she was beat to it.

"Well now, here we are, at another time and another venue. Care to reconvene?"

"I can't, I'm out."

"I'm sorry, what..."

"You are less dominant attractive with the apologies." said Colleen.

"Careful, your little tush is cruising for a bruising and the cloth of that dress ain't gonna give cushion for the wrath the person attached to that ass will experience."

"It's my ass, I can subject it to what ever I may desire."

She reached forward with her other hand and caressed my cheek, I reached up and caressed her hand. Which was when she said while shaking her head, her face bearing a disappointed look, with frisky blended in, "No, no, sweetie your ass doesn't belong to you any more, it's mine now, you see."

I shivered, shuddered and was getting aroused with only the banter and the rather intimate but acceptable displays of affection. Keep it together Colleen, back on mission.

"So why did you say you were out earlier?"

"Well, now we both are," Colleen said with a mischievous grin, counting the seconds in her head. And then seeing the recognition set in.

Her nameless crush hung her head and muttered, "Shit." Then she looked up and stated, "But you have one question left."

"I don't feel so, well, maybe, I assumed we were at another venue and at a later time as I walked up to your table. Now maybe you didn't even know it was me at the time but, I asked my question already. So I see it that now we're both question broke." And I was smirking again with the shear ecstasy of it, while hoping for more wrath to my derrière to later ensue.

"Remind me."

"No."

"Remind me, now."

I twisted my head up and to the left, placed a pointed index under my chin.

"Hmmm, No."

"Colleen, your Mistress has given you an order, twice now but, just so we are clear, defy your Mistress again at that ass's peril and I'll also remind you, it's now my property. Remind me."

"Oh, okay, all right and fine, if that's the way it is, then..." I left it seconds to simmer, then playfully spat out, "No."

"Colleen." She growled playfully "You're going to be screaming my name later. Final warn... shit."

I had my hand over her mouth, biting my everything I had to bite. Lower lip and tongue sandwiched between incisors and molars on inside of both cheeks just trying not to roar out loud with laughter but I'm certain it came through in my eyes, just looking at my crush with all that suppressed laughter. "And your name is?"

"Veronica." She said, looking away with what seemed sincere frustration and defeat.

"Permission to touch my Mistress?"

"Granted."

"I'm always winning, but most especially if and when those wins are at the expense of me in sufferance to your admonishments and punishments." I finished, with a caress of my own under my Mistress Veronica's chin, while gently drawing her face and sight line back in my direction. "Mistress Veronica." I stated as our eyes once again met.

They both would have grinned at each other for another several minutes if not for a female groan behind them.

They both looked to see the blond behind the bar with a playful yet scornful look just as she stated, "You both need to get a room, we're linked to a hotel so it'll be super easy, I can deal with a lot. But right now, I'd like you both chained up in my basement and there being a lot of my own cruelties in retaliation for what you both are putting me through over here."

The fuse lit was short, the explosion of laughter from all three of them was near simultaneous. The bar was empty except for the three of them. But it felt as though they would have laughed all the same. And just as hard if it was over capacity with all thejudgmental beings of the world pressed in like sardines.

I was gaming out a scenario involving my Mistress Veronica and the somewhat portly but cute wench who I had checked over earlier when my jaw dropped at what was said next.

"Well now our fair wench, this little bitch has extremes coming to her that could get us kicked out of our hotel room, maybe you help me with both the extremes of her torment and the extremes of my pleasure, us being honoured guests in your basement."

"I close up at 12:30, what's your room number, we'll drive back to my place with your little bitch in the trunk." She said with a sadistic smile, throwing a wink at Colleen.

"Colleen! What do you say!?" Veronica barked.

My voice was a trembling whisper, "Thank you, Mistresses. I will be worthy, I promise."

When Veronica and Colleen arrived back in their room, Veronica came right out with it, "You feigned being tired, didn't you."

Colleen went over and sat on the bed, looked at Veronica and said, "Yes and no, let's talk." As she patted the bed beside her.

Veronica came over and sat, looking somewhat chagrined, "look, I'm sorr..."

Colleen had slipped up her hand and placed one index finger against her lips with such speed that Veronica had heard the wind wake that her arm had made in travel.

Veronica just looked at her shocked. Then looked at what Colleen had done with her other hand.

She placed it by her own ear and pointing at it with again the index finger and a tapping motion. Then she went through five hand signals, at first the signal, then the motion. And for all of them she, had left Veronica on the bed and acted out what was expected for them.

By the third one Veronica was smiling, she nodded confirmation at the end of each example and showed intent interest.

Once finished Colleen went to her rucksack and pulled out a smartphone from an easily accessible front pocket. She came over and sat beside Veronica sharing the screen between them and rapidly typed out some explanation.

-we go through it quiet in case we are being listened in on
-also because we learn it's about no sound and rapid response, what hand signals are meant for. Example, you see someone in the motion of swinging a golf club at my head from behind me, point to the floor in the direction I should be moving and I trust you know

what I need to do. Scream my name and point behind me, I end up concussed.

-these are for us in the heat of battle, they have worked in survival situations for our species since we understood silence and moving can mean life or death.

-and now I want to put you through the paces, so say what you were going to when we first got in, then we'll talk on it and then I'm going to signal you a situation had arisen. If you don't impress me, I get a spanking for being an ineffective teacher.

Veronica must've been so into the whole of it all that she threw her head back to laugh and kept it silent. Even though all motions in body and expressions in face were there for it. Like she was on mute.

I looked at her in total amazement, then with enough speed to shame a snake, I slid my hand around Veronica's neck and rammed my closed lips into Veronica's still open mouth – no sense in either, or both of us chipping a tooth.

She still had her eyes closed from the head thrown back laugh, they slammed open with exhilaration. Then she moved her tongue outward, but met closed lips. The lips stayed pressed into her open mouth but denied her tongue entry, she pushed, they clamped tighter and pushed back more, left than right, tongue flicking like a lizard. And then she realized, this woman of mine has such propensity for being a difficult submissive, it should never be underestimated. She doesn't have it in spades, she has it in all the spades of all the card decks in the whole world. Probably a few decks that haven't been made yet owe her a few as well.

Colleen squealed out, "You cheater!" Though it was muffled by their mouths still being one. Her lip defences had however failed, she was being tickled by eager little fingers from both hands of her Mistress. All while being tongued with fury in her mouth. She ended up being chased down to the bed on her back, an eternity in that kiss would be a good use of time and an easy way to spend it. The tickling on the other hand would require being in bondage for duration viability.

Veronica suddenly wrenched up by pushing down on her subby's little tummy. This girls abs feel to be composed of rock or steel. "On your feet, bend over and place your hands on that wall, now!"

Colleen looked shocked for the blink of an eye, then ecstatic.

Veronica hadn't missed it, nor the raising of Colleen's dress to just allow the slightest view of her pubic mound swelling the crotch of her thong.

Then Colleen put on a solemn and pouty face, getting up and assuming the position.

Veronica rolled across the bed, both as quickly and quietly as possible, the implement of her desire was handle up, sticking out of the bag. Just as she had planned for and prepped it that way, she looked over her shoulder and smiled. Her form in that dress is perfect, I hate her hips for how well she makes it look. One thing missing. "Spread your legs bitch!"

I complied somewhat shuffling, the four-point-five heels I still wore, made the act of standing with spread legs a tad challenging. I was quivering with anticipation and the feel of air openly flowing across my cloth'd over vagina and bare skin. Me being well aware of this dress having ridden up. I feel exposed. I feel nasty. I feel alive!

Veronica dragged out the appreciation of the view for as long as she dared and then rolled over pressing into a leap from the bed. She executed a perfect Kendo strike, with both hands on the handle of the paddle, the impact landing on Colleen's right ass cheek.

"AAHHIIEEEEE!!!" I screamed at the ceiling having thrown my head back. I then felt a chin rest on my shoulder and a deliberate blow of air against my neck just under my ear. Then I heard the nearly inaudible whisper.

"You bad, bad girl. Less kissy kissy, more teachy, teachy. What happens if we get in a life or death situation and I get a hangnail because of your inability to remain professional. I'll tell you what happens, I drive that hangnail into your nipple as a piercing. Now, shall we try again."

"Yes Mistress." Aaargh! I yell as my hair is yanked back.

"Mistress whom?!"

"Yes, Mistress Veronica, thank you, Mistress Veronica for your astute observation and your correctional methods."

"Are you mocking me slut, because if you are..."

"No, Mistress, never, Mistress, thank you, Mistress." Just as I finished, I heard the sigh of frustration and quickly added, "Mistress Veronica."

"Hmm... well, I'm not letting it slide, but I'm also not going to take it out of your left cheek just yet." Live in fear, my little Colleen."

"Yes, Mistress Veronica, thank you, Mistress Veronica." I said while she gnawed on my ear and breathed on my neck.

Veronica quickly withdrew and went to sit on the bed again.

I stayed where I was and as I was. Less out of fear of reprisal, more for the erotic aspect of not moving without permission. Gee willikers, my ass is sore.

"Colleen, come sit with me."

"Yes, my Queen." I said with total sincerity, but also to playfully test the waters.

"My Queen? My, my, I like that. How about we have our own little signals and signs worked out at some point so we can switch things on and off. I guess the signal for when you want your mistress being activated is easy enough, just do and say all those things that make me want to put you over my knee. But for now..." she raised the paddle she held and twirled it. "We'll, get back to the basic training.

Colleen went over to her duffle and pulled out some pants, a long-sleeved shirt and returned to the bed. Only briefly scrunching up her face and flinching when her ass made contact with the bed. "Yeesh! What the hell and where the hell?" She motioned to the paddle with the wad of clothes she held.

"Remember what we both wanted and the verbal collision that happened when we got here? I'm guessing you wanted to go dress shopping, and thank you, sincerely. That effort on your part and the result made this a night to remember. Even in full onset dementia or severe brain damage. Anywho, I had seen an adult toy store on our ride here from the airport and absolutely had to go accessorize. And as to what," she flipped it around to show the other side had a protruding backward word four letters long. "If it works as advertised I'm looking forward to seeing you change into your ninja black clothes you have there."

"Well, you are welcome for the dress and you are welcome to see me shed it and everything I'm wearing. I did spend forty dollars of yours for the heels."

"Well, I own you now so, no worries on you owing me," Veronica said mischievously with a face to match.

Just words and expressions from my Veronica have me totally twitterpated. "Also, thank you, sincerely, for going accessorizing for us. You are also welcome to these." I added, handing them to my Veronica.

"For me! Ninja clothes! You shouldn't have, um, they feel like they've gotten too much starch?"

"I know, they don't look like much..."

"No, hey, I'm not complaining, I just..."

"As I was explaining before being so rudely interrupted, remember now, less talk'y, talk'y, more listen, listen."

Veronica made a 'I'm shutting up now' gesture with pursed lips and said nothing.

"They are double layered ultra-high molecular weight polyethylene with a third outer layer of hemp. I have them custom made every once in a while. My sizes on you may be a tad loose and like wearing a circus tent. However you'll be tactically prepared for diving into a slide on rough surfaces and any sort of sharps' encounters as you can be. While just wearing pants and a shirt anyway."

"Sharps' encounters?"

"Ya, broken glass, edged weapons attacks, hell, even a hacking heavy blade like an axe or machete may cause less deep tissue damage. This is because it will actually need a sawing like back and forth motion just to cut through the inner two layers. And that's if it's sharp, the outer layer of hemp is pretty tough in itself. Well, any way, I just want you to be as well protected as possible, with the proper gear and knowledge." I was looking down at the floor, kind of embarrassed when I heard the thick fabric settle on the bed. Then felt the arms wrap around me in a hug.

"You're truly awesome, my little socio, and don't let anyone tell you different. I'll wear them and feel safer thinking of you, but, what about you? I want you safe as possible, and you won't be with me wearing your combat clothes."

"I have four more sets in my duffle, we should change into them now." Colleen went to rise and then stopped. She put her hand on Veronica's left leg and said nothing for a while.

"What, what's wrong?"

Colleen squeezed her leg and seemed to have trouble saying what she wanted to.

"Hey, no pressure or judgment, just honesty, remember." Veronica said, finishing with a hand placement on Colleen's bare thigh and a friendly little shake.

"Okay, no offence but, here's how it is. If I had two weeks to train you and you were dedicated to it, we could cross paths with three guys well out of our weight class and size. I'd deal with my two, never once being concerned about you handling your own. Hell, you've surprised me a lot already, maybe I'm not giving you enough credit and you'd be fine with your own two. However, until I've had some time to show you how to GTW, sorry, Go To War with another human being, when it comes to us at risk, I'm in charge. No questions, no doubts, I need to know that you will leave me and not look back if the situation calls for it."

Veronica's hand went to her mouth, her eyes were starting to moisten, she could not have known till this point that this tough little broad had become so fond of her, so much, in such a little amount of time. She didn't have to look at the clock to confirm that they had a few hours over twenty four in which they actually had known each other. She got up and started stripping to don her new clothes. At this point, it was the only answer she was ready to give.

Colleen watched her Veronica moving to change and took some solace in the fact that she would be as safe as possible for now. If I had force fields from the future and other advanced technology protecting her, I still would feel the need for more security for my Queen.

I got up and strolled over to the full length mirror to once again take in my appearance in this type of garb I had never wanted to wear before. Not for any reason or anybody, before the last twenty-six hours, twenty-one minutes and thirty-eight seconds, thirty-nine seconds, forty sec... Colleen, stop, just stop.

6

"Spanking for your thoughts, hon."

Colleen heard the phrase at the same moment a chin rested on her shoulder and a face nuzzled into her neck and the lower regions of one of her neck's erogenous zones.

She leaned into that face and reined herself in. She was after all, ready and willing to jump this women in the throes of passion. On the bed just behind them, if they made it that far. We'd thrash and roll, bite and scratch, be all over, around and in each other so much as to put a weasel orgy to shame. If they have orgies, that is.

"Before, you nuzzling into me, they were about this dress and how it was never important for me before today, for no reason or another person." I heard my Veronica's breath catch and smiled. "And then once you were nestled in on my shoulder, weasel orgies."

"Weasel orgies?"

"I'll let you suffer with the anticipation of my explaining my thought process of that hypothetical situation. For now, if my Mistress likes, as you suggested you can sit and watch me strip."

Veronica kissed my neck, and walked back to the bed and sat.

I'm so glad that kiss was as simple as it was and she stayed the hell away from my earlobe. I could have refrained from tearing us up in rough and tumble weasel-wrestling sex, but I probably, definitely would not have. All our enemies coulda busted in and I'd carry on.

As smoothly and sensually as I'd ever tried for, I lost everything but the heels. Then quickly grabbed my phone, bent over sexy and took a mirror selfie. Another I'd never do in a million. Evaluated the snap and handed it to my Veronica. Even reversed, I realized what the paddle said. What I now seen reversed again thanks to the mirror. MINE. I'm only too glad to be hers. "We'll get a print out of it and have it framed for you. The way some townie proud new owners of their property get photos of their new possessions."

Veronica was admiring the photo and it became evident how much she was when she replied, "Huh? Sorry hon, you caught me not listening."

Colleen just smiled and shook her head as she turned, bent and pulled out her own combat ready attire.

Veronica was all about the view, her subject, the pose, the four letter word perfectly legible in red welt on its perfect backdrop. Could I ever be so happy, as to know it true? That she could be mine? Colleen was dressed entirely too fast for her liking and lacing up boots in a strange method she had never seen. Manipulating both loops at the same time, one in each hand. "Say, babe, would it reassure you any if I've been an avid studier of a martial art? And I've actually been advanced ahead several times. Well ahead of typical timelines, my instructor says my dedication isn't what people usually put in."

"Kendo is a fine example of a deadly art, a Shinai swung lightly can break bones." Colleen replied matter-of-factly.

"Is it a psychic thing with you? Because, at times you really are a freaky little ninja chick."

Retracting her left hand from her rucksack rummage, Colleen used it to point at the mirror. "I seen your attack with the paddle on my ass. It was very fine form." She turned back facing Veronica, with two objects in her hand, metal tubes.

Veronica was smiling and looking at her, a perfect amalgamate of admiration and fascination.

"That's why I thought you may be right at home with these."

"Oh my gosh! Those are extending batons!"

"Yup, but, again, a creation of my own design, they have extra length and are spring loaded. The trigger requires a two-to-three pound impact on the back end." She spun one around and flowed to the floor in a crouch. In a coordinated hammer blow to the carpeted floor, the baton had shot out in length. She handed it extended to Veronica.

Veronica stood, took it in a two handed grip, like one holds a sword with hilt to accommodate both. Doing a thrust to a parry and then a flowing three-slice pattern, left to right, like fluid, she executed the return back to the left and then equally gracefully, transitioned to the overhead attack down on a shadow enemy. "It's good, I like the weight, the balance is fine and it may only be an inch shy of what I'm used to for sparring. Just want you to show me other options for opening it besides dropping to a crouch, I don't much like the idea of cowering before engaging.

Colleen nodded. "You're familiar with using the hilt of a sword for attack, yes?"

"Oh! Of course, a pommel strike. I guess we aren't worried about fouls with these ass-hats. And then I just position myself off side of my blade as if it were there! I'm sorry, I could have figured that out."

"No worries, an implement you aren't familiar with can set you back to beginner territory quite often. But once you are familiar, hell, I have no doubt you may show me a new thing or two. For example, imagine facing off with a jerk and you have one behind you. Use either dipshit as your backing for the trigger, just make damn sure to be off to the side like you said. These things spring extend with more than enough force to cause serious injury. Also, timing it right for distance will cause your backing board a painful Yawara blow and with the necessary aim, a worse blow to the other." Colleen handed her the yet-to-be-triggered baton in exchange for the triggered one. And watched her go through some motions with spot-on form.

"Coolio, show me something else with em."

Colleen used the already extended baton, showed her an imagination of the baton she held yet to be extended. Then said, "Don't knock the idea of cowering," as she ducked down in a scared body language position, now see where I am with baton position for deployment?" Gently tapping the end of the baton two to three inches above Veronica's bottom of crotch.

"Oh my goodness, you are not a nice person if someone motivates you to be so."

Colleen smiled, evaluated the distance and then hooked her baton handle end in behind Veronica's calf and pushed in the top of baton at her lower abdominal.

Veronica had trust fallen on the bed and seen Colleen flow upward and on top of her. Coming to rest with her baton just above Veronica's throat, still held in both hands at opposing ends.

"And you roll with your opponent as they fall, rolling over top of them off to the side. Even rolling over an adversary, with your forearm down across their windpipe can be fatal."

Veronica just lay there looking into Colleen's eyes as if she wanted to say something.

"What?" Colleen asked.

"It's stupid, even more stupid if we can't see it as a joke."

"Try me."

Veronica blinked, as to bat her eye lashes and painted smitten all over her face, "Marry me."

Colleen rolled her eyes, pushed off the bed, turning away while simultaneously letting out a friendly frustrated, "Baaahhgh." Then turned back, also looking somewhat smitten at her Veronica laying there.

The laughter that broke out between them was so in-tune, they could have been one entity laughing at the whole of existence.

They had pretty much trained, learned from and taught each other up until the time their honourable and revered wench would be closing up shop. Colleen had stopped things, taken care of preparations and covered how it would go when the knock at the door came. When Mandy did knock, Colleen had her smart phone in camera mode, crouched below the peep hole and lined up the lens with that of the door viewer. There stood their new friend on the screen of Colleen's phone.

Veronica mouthed the letters "O and K" with the question on her face.

Colleen shook her head in the negative. She reached for Veronica's hand, brought it up to the phone and she took over holding it over the peep hole. Colleen was in and out of her rucksack, and had returned to the door with Paracord in seconds. She cast a look at Veronica who was off to the side of their door.

Veronica knew the plan, they had talked on the hypothetical of Mandy being of help to others against her will. She didn't like it but, had promised she was going to do as Colleen asked. Observation only and possibly a snatch and grab of Mandy out of the hall. But only under the parameters Colleen had set forth. So she watched and waited.

Colleen had rented two rooms, vacancy was high so it was easy to get them across from each other. It was also easy to get the one room as vacant with no name on the register. Because Colleen's appearance was already altered, she handled the acquisition of the rooms alone. My sister had to get out, blah, blah, her abusive husband, blah, blah. And the manager behind the desk being female made the process really silky.

Colleen had instructed her to comply with any scary scenario and bring up the hotel register and room occupancy if asked. Yes there is a woman matching that description, she is in room 117.

The room that Colleen just lowered into, in the bathroom, from the overhead ducting. She set to task and was ready to open the door in less than a minute. Most of the work was already done.

Mandy had never been more scared in her life. The two men that came into the bar 20 minutes before last call had somehow known that she lied. They had sat at the bar, ordered beers and then produced a photo of the dominant woman. "Never seen her before." Was Mandy's reply. Maybe she would've been more convincing if she had never gotten to know those two. Even the little she had interacted, they both seemed to be decent people. Maybe these bastards seen her concern about them when she first looked at the image. All she did know is the guy with his hand on the door's handle side had a gun pointed at her gut. And then she heard the indications of a hotel door about to be opened. Mandy closed her eyes, part in shame and part to trap the tears, but one escaped confinement.

Harkly had been employed by these spooky bastards for around five years. He kept longing to get killed on one of these jobs. It seemed a better option than to succumb to any of the horrors he and others had heard were dealt by those above them. Those whose only sin was not delivering success where failure was not an option if you want to avoid a miserable death. Hey, it damn sure made people want to measure up, or die trying. He always took the door hinge side. The logistics of being shot on handle side just weren't there. But hinge side had those. Maybe today is my lucky day.

The two men were flattening themselves against the wall on either side of the door. Mergan looked to his partner and nodded, they had both heard the door handle activating. Mergan had only been on the job with Harkly for a month, and it was okay for the most part. He trusted him enough, but the worry was in Harkly not seeming steadfast. You want to do this kind of work, you have to be that. Whatever, go time he thought. We kill this broad, set the scene with the bartender and then kill her. Home in time for my television programs.

The problem came when the door opened and no one was in sight. Both Harkly and Mergan had nearly the same thoughts about it. Eerie, these are heavy and piston pressured auto closure. They don't open by themselves, and they don't stay open by themselves.

Mandy just stood there, terrified and eyes closed. She heard the door sweep over the commercial carpet and expected the shooting any second now and her death shortly there after. A fleeting thought of holding her son again made what she thought to be her last breath catch in her throat– an audible gasp. I would have liked to smell his hair one last time.

Veronica watched the trembling Mandy, watched the door swing all the way open to a seemingly empty room and watched the two goons looking confused. After hand signalling their actions, they went to work, the one went high, the other low. They both had silenced pistols aimed into the room, one crouched and the other standing. Nothing but silence and stillness.

Colleen just stayed in her position, biding her time. Having seen what she had, she knew the men were trained, experienced and had seen violence. She smiled, because she was, had and witnessed all that herself as well. I have every intention of being chained up in a basement and tormented later this morning. So I'm gonna get this all dealt with like I always have before. She held position and waited.

The two men saw the room's distant lamp was on, making it well lit but still throwing shadows for concealment. They both eyed each other and then Mergan moved further forward. This time, Mergan took the risks, sweeping into the room and trusting his partner to cover the bathroom. Harkly held the door, staying in arm's reach of the bartender and hung back from stepping fully inside the room. Though he didn't know it, he was still too far in for his own good.

Colleen just kept her position, back pressed up into the ceiling, feet stretched out with her legs straight, ankles extended and arms bent at the elbows near the inside wall corners. So when she snapped her feet flat and rapidly extended her arms straight applying traction pressure to the wall her palms pressed into, her legs started to drop before the rest of her. She glided down just off to the side of the man's arm and pistol. He had no chance.

Veronica was still not within the parameters for dragging Mandy clear but she had her hand on the door handle of the room she watched from. Staying at the ready. Still watching the screen, she found the best grip to hold the phone while clamping it in position against the door. She had perfect view of Mandy's back and the open door to the other room because the doors across from each other were hardly offset. So when the action commenced, she missed nothing. But discerned little, all blurs of fast motion and it seemed like an event that couldn't be measured in full seconds.

Harkly talked a lot of shit to himself about dying on the job but training takes over and you still fight on, he wasn't doing well. One second he was watching Mergan clear the typical corner a hotel room has, created by the wall for the bathroom. The next a figure was standing off to his right, dainty, female? The palm to his temple really hampered his ability to evaluate such things. If that wasn't enough, the finger drag into his right eye was quite the effective addition. Then he felt his gun arm wrenched towards his partner and knew he wasn't doing well. The finger over his finger on the trigger, the recoil of his pistol, once, twice and a then a third. Not well, definitely not well at all.

Colleen had placed her first shot, second and third right where she wanted, were they really hers, yeah, they were. Even without holding the fire arm she had total control of aim and discharge. She put no more time into the prick that was shot, he was all done. Well, he did still have decomposing to do and now to finish with my dance partner.

Mandy had opened her eyes to a blur of motion. At the first shot, she realized a gun was no longer pointed at her. At the second shot, she dropped and crab-crawled backwards cowering against the room door directly behind her. Leaning into it, she fell back when it opened and would have fallen all the way if not for the hands that caught her. She didn't fully comprehend the order barked in a whisper.

Veronica had dropped the phone in the waste basket filled with bathroom towels by the door and yanked on the handle. The way Mandy crumpled into the door, it appeared she had been hurt. When Veronica seen the woman was falling in, she caught her under the arms and whispered loudly in her ear. "Get in here!"

Colleen had a dance partner with a ringing head, incapacitated vision and an arm that was twisted two ways, both being all wrong for a gentle spin. But all right for a hard slam into the stereotypical hotel desk. Colleen frowned in concern, the desk looked unwell. She was sure it wasn't going to make it. Still the universe's agent for balance, still fully operational. Well for sector earth anyway. In the small corner of it, when and where she inhabited what ever corner at whenever. She had every intention of continuing to remain so.

With pistol aimed she stood on her dance partner's hand, serious weight and then ground out a cigarette that wasn't there. He's out or a damn good tolerator of pain. Even so she kept peripherals on him and moved to the other guest they had for the evening. He couldn't fake the bullet hole at the base of his neck. That hole didn't bode well for the brain stem that connected to spinal cord. Maybe our dearly departed desk would be his first furniture in the afterlife. Don't think he deserved such a steadfast flat surface though, or an afterlife.

She had acquired more Paracord and secured Mr. "Can't Dance" with his hands tied in front in short order. Came to the open door and the hallway, peeked out left then right and was satisfied the hall was clear. Only then did she remove the rope from the door handle that had opened the door with the weight of the dresser as a counterweight. Colleen stepped into the hall and closed the room door behind her. Took two steps across the hall without breaking stride, as the door was opening with the perfect timing of a world famous orchestrator. She walked into a powerful hug from Veronica.

"I'm glad you are you," Veronica said into Colleen's ear.

Colleen replied, "I'm glad you're glad." She broke from the embrace. "Okay ladies, cold hard facts time. First, we're clearing out in two minutes or less. Second I'd like to chat with the one who's still alive with that remaining time and it most likely won't be a nice chat."

Both women looked at Colleen with expressions that Colleen expected, then nodded their understanding once each.

"Okay, Veronica, pack us up, load into Mandy's car and have it sitting outside the fire door at the end of this hallway." Colleen turned to

Mandy. "Sorry about use of your car but I'm not asking, I'm telling." With key card already in gloved hand, Colleen turned and walked out across and in. As she suspected the door handle striker was still held flush in the open position by the hotel notepad she placed against the doorframe on her way out. Having the key ready was just a good idea, both for the just in case and for appearances.

A quick search of the two men told Colleen a lot. She moved on, giving a kick to the trussed up man, more to hurry things along than out of cruelty. If necessary, cruelty comes later. She collected up everything in twenty seconds, and had it on her person neat and tidy in about the same. Leaving her a minute for small talk.

***

Colleen walked down the hall towards the fire exit, some cut lengths of Paracord she twisted and squeezed. What he told her was motivating the abuse of the useless lengths. His end at his own hand was both a relief at the time but of immense concern now. None of it mattered. She had thought of turning the opposite way in the hall, never seeing her Veronica again. The thought hadn't been long enough to plague her with indecision.

None of it mattered because Veronica deserved a chance. Everyone does, she thought. I give that one chance to everyone when it comes to truth. Exercise it with me or say goodbye to me, I write off anyone who can't level with me. Even with the small things if you can't trust with the little ones, you probably can't trust with the big ones either. Please, please, please be honourable, tell me everything and it won't matter what that everything is. If the truth was that she had made enemies with all of hell's occupants, it's all good. My first thoughts, okay, so what ring of hell do I wage war on first? Is there strategic benefit to it if I start at one, or seven or just drop in the middle and blitzkrieg it all until I win or lose. I'd do all that, just be honest with me.

At the end of her long walk down the hall she pushed open the steel security door causing the alarm to sound and stepped into the waiting car that promptly drove off. She wasn't fuming, her emotions were all in check. Except the one that until today was never of concern to her, she'd never visited this uncharted territory of caring before. Colleen was afraid, afraid of the loss, and it was a loss guaran-damnteed without truth.

From the back seat, Veronica watched a robot calmly exit the door, slide into the car through the waiting open front door and then saw the creature sit there like an inanimate object. She was terrified, of only one thing. Never seeing her Colleen ever again, that what they had was no longer. Because her Colleen was no longer hers to have. She looked away out the window at the components of a city as the car passed them all by. I don't deserve her anyway, I never did.

7

Mandy pulled her car into a driveway, parked, shut it off and oddly put both hands on the wheel again. She faltered to draw them out. "I'll.. I will... gonna go in and, uh... make some tea."

"Tea would be great, we will be right in," replied Colleen.

Mandy nodded, and sat there for another minute. As if she couldn't shift her hands from the ten and two positions on the steering wheel. Eventually she nodded once, seemed to remove her hands as if fighting some attractive force from the wheel, slowly got out and then made her way to the house.

Veronica and Colleen sat in silence.

Colleen knew it had to be up to her. "Veronica, even if you don't join us inside, if this was the last time I ever saw you, I have no regrets about our encounter, never had and never will. I'll see to it there is a cup set out for you and hope it's not done for nothing."

Veronica met Colleen's eyes in the rear view.

They held such sorrow, it seemed, at any time they could have wept for every sadness that had ever been. Mirrors, the only object of our creation that can show emotion, in reflection. Colleen wasn't staring her down. She tried with her whole being to look out with eyes of understanding, compassion and void of any judgment. But Colleen couldn't look away. If this is my last look into my Veronica's eyes and I look away... then I'll walk on damned for eons.

Veronica held her gaze, then nodded and got out of the car.

Colleen followed but then walked up to the house with out looking back.

Later Colleen looked out through a front window into the darkness of night. Hours ago the three of them had sat holding cups of tea for enough time for it to be past ridiculous without taking a drink. Colleen had been the one to break the silence. She broke it with her stoic talent of handling any direness, truly to this point, any, with no emotion whatsoever unless it was actually of benefit. Which was rare to never in her opinion.

First, she was concerned about the safety of Mandy, and anyone connected to her. Colleen may have found it spooky that the entire surveillance system of the hotel had been down. However, she defined coincidence as pattern. Just my cosmic forces employers saying what they say. According to Mandy the chance of any of them being connected via recorded image was zero. It had to do with primary tech for the recording system burning out. A mere seven hours before my Veronica and I were even aware of where we would be next. She was so glad to have just thought that – still her Veronica. Yet again the universe seeming to see merit in Colleen's continued endeavours. Even offering tech support. Anything you need Colleen, we are here to help.

The two of them had talked after Mandy had gone off to bed. It was clearly on no one's agenda for basement mischief. The talk had started in point form like narrative.

"Was the talk as not nice as you expected?"

"I was surprised it stayed nicer than some I've had."

"Did he say much?"

"Very little but..."

"But?"

"What little it was and what he offered spoke volumes." She then relayed the two sentences required to brief Veronica. "'You have no way of understanding what your up against, I don't even know the magnitude of it but I know this, I would rather make enemies with any other organization that deals in death than the one I used to work for.'"

"Then he raised up his gun I held, bit down on the silencer and flicked the trigger."

Veronica's only reply was hanging her head, plunging her face down into waiting hands.

Colleen waited. Continued to wait. And then waited some more. Until Veronica's voice, under such strain that Colleen expected to sense the non-visible words snap as she heard them.

"Well, you see why I tried to talk you into walking away when you were in my bedroom."

"Yes, I do have an understanding of that now. But what about now."

"What?"

"Here we are now, that was then. What about now?"

"Oh, well, the same sentiment, I guess. Yeah, I still want you to leave me and get clear if it's not too late." Her hands had dropped, her head still low, she looked at her lap.

"Too damn bad."

Veronica coughed, more of a shock response. Then slowly raised her head.

When their eyes met, Colleen again witnessed in them what seemed sorrow immeasurable. "I know of only one way I would ever walk away from you. If you hold back, if you choose to not be forthcoming with me, just tell me Veronica. If you can do that, tell me what you are facing here, you won't be facing it alone. No matter what it is you're up against, I'll be at your shoulder and we'll be up against it together."

"Why?"

"Don't be dumb."

Veronica stifled a laugh. "I want to believe the why you would stand by me, that I mean that much to you."

"Forget belief systems, you can look at that as fact and know it to be so."

"Yes, there was a bit of that in the why but I was also asking why it's so important to you that I spill all."

"First and foremost?" Colleen asked.

Veronica nodded.

"Survival is how my brain is primarily wired or it's how I've rewritten over modernized world living progr... whatever, none of that matters. Survival, yours and mine, plain and simple. I can't be effective if I'm operating on partial awareness of a situation."

"That's it?"

"No, how I may pass judgment on anyone, yourself included and probably the only way is if there is honesty lacking in a person, lies, or deceit. If one person chooses what not to divulge to another, no matter what the truth is and how horrible, I don't believe there is greater respect or disrespect a person can show to another."

"I'm scared."

"Of what?"

"What you'll think of me."

"I've done all I can to convey that I'll think more of you if you discard that fear."

"Okay, but when I'm done. If you did think less of me or wanted to think of me not at all and ever again, I'll understand."

Later as Veronica slept, Colleen stood in front of the curtained window and through a small gap in fabric meeting looked into the darkness, feeling at ease with the view. All the details of their conversation ran through Colleen's mind. "It's a death sentence, Colleen, having this organization for an enemy." Sounds like a challenge to me. Colleen stared out the window, hearing her Veronica breathe. It was calm now but before Colleen had been tormented by what ever subconscious brain activity had tormented Veronica. Once, Colleen even wanted to wake her. She refrained and simply took her hand, held it and thought to herself I'd dive right in there and make those torments mine if I could. She smiled at the memory of how Veronica seemed to calm instantly, moaned softly and then snored peacefully. Is that a quirk I need to learn to tolerate or will she be okay with me wearing earplugs when we sleep alongside each other?

Colleen had heard it all, shocked Veronica with her matter-of-fact sentiment to it and even earned herself admonishments. She smirked, her favourite was, "Colleen, you can't be that stupid!"

The syndicate. Which one. The one that all the others would cross the street to avoid, if they knew about it that is. Colleen mulled that over. It was a nice analogy. Only a few of the oldest and largest syndicates were on negotiating level with them but they weren't aware of their existence either. Then there was the being guaranteed the shorter end of the stick in any accords.

"So there is a top dog." Colleen muttered to herself. "There always is. Even in our beginnings as a species, who can kick crap outta every one else was always a part of our hierarchy. Top dog, we're still so devolved, how we come this far let alone go farther with the proliferation of our species is beyond me. At least back when it was grunts and growls between us there was a point. Powerful ruled for the good of the group, it was about survival, not about the material." The soft voice interrupted Colleen talking to herself.

"You talk to yourself a lot. That's kinda weird."

"You're weird."

"No, you are. Definitely."

"Sorry for the audio version of it, it's what goes through my head all the time, when I'm awake."

"I rest my case, weirdo. So have you and yourself come up with any strategies?"

"I run 'em all to ground, destroy them all and we live happily ever after. That's my favourite so far."

"Jeez, you're dumb. I like the last bit though."

"Look, I've been building a little cabin out in the middle of nowhere. It has no services, we'd be living as rustic as those who first lived in these lands but, if we could get there with no trail to follow us. They'd be looking forever and to no ends."

"So, where would I poop?"

"Away from our source of water, at least two hundred feet is... were you joking?"

"Of course I was. The serious questions are, where do I plug in the Magic Wand and the Sybian for your forced orgasms when we have no electricity?"

Colleen smirked, "Ya, that part of our rustic existence would suck."

"Hey, thanks for sticking around. Showing me my fear of losing you was unfounded."

"Don't breathe too easy, your fear wasn't that unfounded..." as soon as Colleen witnessed her shocked look and mouth open she finished with, "When I find you with air conditioning and extra cup holders, you are on a lot collecting dust for all I care!"

"You bitch!" Veronica whisper yelled while failing horribly to look genuinely mad and flung her pillow at me.

I caught it with ease and made a show of plumping it as I walked over. Upon arrival I gently caressed the back of my Mistress's neck, gentler still lifted her head and put the pillow under. "You should try and get some more sleep. We are guests here and you are being childish. Maybe it's because my wittle Vewanica is still tywerd—YEEEOUCH!!!"

Veronica had reached up through the thin blanket and found both of my nipples, squeezed and twisted mercilessly.

"What did you say to me, Colleen!?"

I so cherish the way she makes my name sound when she sneers its pronunciation the way she does. "I'm sorry, Mistress Veronica! Maybe it's me who is short on sleep and not behaving!"

"And...?"

"Thank you for your attentions to me, Mistress Veronica!" Her grip let up about half. If I built cabinets, I could use her hands for clamps on joints... with Clamping Cauls, wouldn't want her leaving finger dents in the oak, yeesh!.

"I just don't know if our relationship will work in rustic conditions. I think you'll always require constant corrections. I'm thinking electricity, to sensitive areas and again with the forced orgasms to extremes will be necessary for maintaining tolerable behaviour."

She had me overcome with arousal by the time we heard Mandy speak.

"You both lick, you both lick so bad," from the entry into the living room.

"I'm making breakfast, if you two are interested and can separate hands from nipples that is. Or come and join me while still pinching em, that works too." She walked out, her barked laughter fading.

I fell into Veronica's chest with my face and in a muffled voice, spoke from the valley of her breasts, "If I still need more correction in your opinion, you could make me eat on all fours out of a dish on the floor, if you wanted."

My Veronica broke out laughing, a laugh that transformed into playful darkness. Accentuated by a smirk that read as pure sin, a facial expression and a, "You're in trouble" tint to her eyes that made me shiver. Then she pushed me back but also down. Grabbed my hair as if to make a pony tail, but tracked down its length until she had a handful of it at the end. Stood and started walking, "Heel, you beautiful bitch!"

I scampered behind on hands and knees to keep up.

8

Sellkritch was fuming and had been doing so for four consecutive hours since Sands left the estate. Though Sands was true to his word. Adhering to his ordered parameters to operate by, Sellkritch received his calls on the hour. It didn't help his rage. Maybe a little, having someone he could rely on out there tracking down the girl. His only solace was to mind-drift to times past, when honour was still a constant. Not the type to lie to himself and claim what he had built with those twelve and attaining what they had now while remaining completely honourable.

Everyone trades their honour for something, for some, all or most of it becomes expendable. He had known one man who seemed worthy of such a high appraisal, the opposite of everyone. It was hard to think about, it was the closest he had ever come to feeling a kinship to another human. The man had literally saved his life twice. Once, when he stood up to Sellkritch. He stood right in front of me and had the courage to tell me a truth. I wanted to kill him for having done so. Brazen, honourable sonofabitch.

The second time he shoved me aside and took two rounds centre mass. To make more of a blood debt, the man stayed behind as a diversion for the police. Didn't die though, he's serving 25 years. Fuck.

Not wanting to think on it any more, he rose up and walked over to a decorative glass top cabinet. His eyes captured glimmers of light from the back-lighting from within. Some of those glimmers were souls laid to rest with the twin three-fifty-seven's that resided within. They only came out for cleaning nowadays and on those occasions, six shots each get fired. But they went into the cabinet and hadn't come out for real use in ten years. Below them were the shoulder holsters and torso harness, which also came out for oil treatments. The equipment in behind the glass had taken care of him for nearly 40 years, seemed wrong to not take care of it in return.

He raised his hands to the lid, gripped and lifted it an inch, then let it settle again. "Not yet," he spoke to the contents. "First we find the girl." Then I'm going back to my old self one last time. Some debts are payable only in blood. Beethoven erupted in his pocket. Pulling the phone out and noting the time, he spoke. "You're early."

"Yes sir. We have a possible trail. Some of our associates in the city's nearest airport have been ordered to be on watch for certain events."

"And?"

"There is an event. I decided to call you with what we have. In all probability, the trail could still be cold, but we're on the way to the scene regardless."

"The three other teams?"

"Holding position until we have a better notion."

Sellkritch had raised the lid, the glimmer in his eyes gone, they looked soulless without it. His deathly stare now played over one of the revolvers, the grave gaze followed his fingertips over the barrel.

"I want positive confirmation or elimination of it. How long till you're on site?"

"We're five minutes out, sir."

"I'll stay on the line and get my own first hand. We'll review after."

"Yes sir."

"Sands, one more thing."

"Sir?"

"When we do have a trail heat up, I'll be putting my boots to ground on it."

"Yes sir, I'll organize."

Sellkritch heard the orders given and someone else in the car making a call.

Before Sands and his team made the hotel, there was a knock at the mahogany.

"Enter."

A suited man came through the doors but stopped just holding them.

"Sir, a car is out front, a four man detail is waiting and the helicopter is standing by with flight plan filed."

"Excellent."

The man nodded, backed out and allowed the doors to shut.

Only then did he realize the big revolver was in his left hand, partially raised towards where the man had stood. Sellkritch one-handed, had the cylinder open to him as familiar as a lover. He was excited, his own hands hadn't taken life for a long time. Longer retired than his revolvers. Eleven years ago he strangled a man to death with them.

Sounds of car doors opening, closed doors to the past he reflected on. Then he heard footsteps on hard surfaces. If all goes well, my footsteps will be doing the same. He got it all in stereo.

***

"Evening Darla, we're here to meet with some police officers on premises. Could you direct us?

Sargeant Wendasque, wasn't sure what to expect. In law enforcement for twenty years, never once had she known of anyone being required to liaise with a private investigative firm. Of all the things she'd learned about in her line of work, one was most prevalent. Ain't happened yet don't mean it won't. "So it's happened," she muttered. She'd be more suspicious if it hadn't come down the chain. At the sound of footsteps in the hall, she popped up from where the one guy had bit down on a gun. At least that was what prelim forensics indicated. That was a "yet" phenomenon as well.

She exited the room not sure what to expect. The three men in the hall looked professional, clean cut and motivated. The one in the centre could have done anything where looks were requirement number one. He spoke first.

"I'm Joseph Petrands. The man to my left is Darren Threshton and to my right is Mal Bordenko. We represent 4D Research. We are here on a person's search, retained by the family of a woman believed to have passed through the area."

Joseph Petrands had produced both business card and licence in a fluid, practiced manner. As did his colleagues.

Wendasque looked over each of their credentials in turn. She had started left and then went right. Finishing with handing Petrands back his ID, she smiled the question, holding up the card. Received a polite smile in return and looked at it while she spoke.

4D

Descry Detect Determine Discover
RESEARCH

"If I wore one, I'd tip a hat to your marketing staff."

Petrands smiled again. Again politely.

Six hundred miles away, Sellkritch smiled. He'd started and named the company two and a half years ago, designed the cards even. Always nice to hear a compliment. His organization had left the corrupting of officials to others early on. Far easier and less risky to hide in plain site. For years, multiple of his house's operatives had valid private investigator licences. When 4D Research was started, it was never thought to be anything but modernizing old tricks. Now it was a 10 million dollar return business. Two offices in his country of residence and another branch opening up overseas in the fall. Go figure.

"Wendasque said it plain. First, I've never had occasion to liaise with a firm like yours before. Second, yes I have been informed of your legitimacy in searching for this woman."

Petrands nodded, delivering his third polite smile.

"And last, I have been authorized to exercise my own discretion on what amount of cooperation will be forthcoming. It's all still by the book. Nothing pertaining to the investigation of crimes committed will be divulged. I don't care how tidy your business cards were laid out."

"Bitch." Sellkritch muttered.

Petrands gave a look that Wendasque read and nodded in response. She was done.

"All is agreeable. We have only maintained amicable interaction with law enforcement because we try to be just that. We hope for our client's sake that this is a false lead. For the woman to be involved with these unfortunate events is not what we want to have to report back. We were hoping for confirmation of her having been in the vicinity, or not. Is there any surveillance footage we could look at, that would be acceptable in your discretion?"

Smooth, too damn smooth. Thought Wendasque. "No, the hotel had issues with the system prior to events taking place here. Unfortunately we are both working blind here. The only staff here have all been interviewed and have nothing relevant to offer. Though we have only interviewed concerning the deceased. We haven't asked about a woman, the woman you are looking to locate. Description?" Wendasque did not divulge the discovery about a short effeminate looking young man securing both the rooms.

"No technical, no sighting. We'll consult with our client." Petrands nodded to Threshton, who withdrew and made a call.

Petrands went through it point by point. Laconic but very on point. Very smooth. "My questions are why you connect events here with the woman you seek?" As well as how you knew of events here in the first place?"

Petrands looked at her with no indication of concern at the heated questions. Then his associate returned and gave a nod. Petrands looked to Bordenko, nodded and turned back to Wendasque. "We have been authorized by our client to involve authorities. We had a possible sighting at an airport one hour from here. Our client is concerned due to past violence, threats and stalking. All of which is on record with the local authorities in the areas of the woman's occupancy. In answer to your last, our sources for information are shown respect of discretion. If ever investigated, our practices would be entirely legal and respectable.

Bordenko had closed his briefcase after removing several photos, handing them forward.

Wendasque reviewed the photos, looked up to none of the men in particular commenting. "She's quite striking." She got no reply except continued professional presentation from the men before her.
"Name, D.O.B., any personal info?"

Petrands gave a finger twirl motion and said. "The subjects particulars are printed on the back of the photos."

Wendasque signalled a uniform over and issued her orders to repeat interviews of any of the staff that were present at the time of incident. "We can only offer you confirmation of a sighting. Nothing will be divulged if the investigation leads to her possible involvement."

Petrands nodded and gave his final polite smile. "A confirmed sighting is our firms only interest. Any involvement of an illegal nature and we report first to the authorities. Then to our client. Which you would save us the trouble. The immediate's particulars will be made available if you desire or require."

Wendasque held up the card, "If I need to contact you?"

"Call the main office number, enter 6-2-4 and ask for me by name. You'll have immediate patch through to my cell. May I get a card, if our firm needs to contact you?"

Wendasque produced one, gave similar instruction and stated. "Gentlemen, I'm on the clock." Turned and reentered the room from which she came. Her mind going over it all. Everything rang true but her instincts said, too damn smooth. But she still couldn't come up with any reason to connect the strangeness of the room rentals or the fatalities to the strangeness of these private investigators. Probably just a coincidence. Wendasque decided she would include it all in her report. However, if she couldn't find any witnesses who could swear to seeing the woman, she would contact the firm and have them relay to Petrands that it is likely a false lead. Just one more thing for me to have on today's docket, I really need a strong coffee.

Sands looked to both men who nodded and went their own directions. He then removed his phone from his front suit pocket as he walked down the hall. He took the phone off speaker and held it to his ear. "Sir?"

"I got it all, no confirmation. That cast-of-stone bitch gave us nothing."

"Not entirely true sir. She gave us audience, a business card and if we are lucky, a list of persons on premises."

"And how do you figure that last part, Sands"

"Associates on it. Call in 23 minutes. Investigating until then."

Selkritch growled down deep where the sound would suffocate, he wasn't in the mood for the propensity Sands had for three or four granule sentences.

"Fine, 23 minutes."

Sellkritch had to admit, his mood wasn't helped by the need for a call he now felt necessary to make. It's not an easy call when the someone you're calling is incarcerated.

Sands knew he wasn't shiny right now, sometimes you have to bear the brunt of it. Giving a man what they want doesn't always make for a felicity. Sands had on more than one occasion bore that brunt, giving his employer what was needed. Results.

Sellkritch had fully proven alias for visitation and phone calls, it had been too long since either. Not only was the man the only he had ever owed, it was the only situation where he contemplated the feeling of guilt. He contemplated this while waiting for a call allowance. When the voice came on from behind a lot of cement and steel, Sellkritch forced the sentiments.

"Hello old friend."

"We are that, old and friends," the man replied.

The pained chuckle of a man who took lead to the chest was hard to hear.

"It's good to hear from you but, why the call."

"We have an issue of obligation. I'm calling in regards to an old debt between us. About that obligation." He knew the cold place was colder now. Not easy news to hear.

"Is it bad? The worst?"

Sellkritch realized he had fumbled things.

"No, not the worst. But there is risk. Location unknown and yes, it's bad."

"I'm in here, won't be getting out, my end of things doesn't matter. I need to know it's honoured, that's all that matters."

Sellkritch kept him waiting longer than he'd have liked. "It's honoured, at my own expense if need be."

"Then I'm okay with what comes. I hope to hear back about it."

"Count on it my friend."

The line cut out. Sellkritch resisted the urge to crush the burner phone to dust. He settled for only cracking the housing and the screen. Then walked over to a painting on the wall, swung it on recessed hinges off the wall and opened an airtight door built into the wall. Then pushed his hand holding the phone into the opening and let gravity take over as the phone slipped from his fingers. With the door left open, the smell of the chemical-filled vat seeped out. As if punishing himself, he let it envelop him until his eyes started to water. When classical music emanated from his pocket, he closed the door and swung the painting back into place.

"Yes." Sellkritch answered

"I have a confirmed sighting. It's not the most respectable of eye whiteness but I substantiate it."

Sellkritch heard a crack come from his primary phone and relaxed his grip.

"Tell me everything."

9

I had a concern about the way things may go, which had nothing to do with limits. I don't really have any. Later that morning I would be going to a local hardware store to acquire the necessaries for us to have some good sessions. Good for my Mistress Veronica and Mistress Mandy. I hope for bad sessions for myself. The hardware store had another benefit for me going, they are good gossip pits. Staff and patrons usually had the latest dirt on the recent ballyhoo.

For the time being however, I was fine with heavy domination with no bondage while being the household's complete submissive. Upon entry to the kitchen in our chosen fashion, Mandy's first response was a predaceous grin. Followed by immediate critique, "I don't think pets should wear clothes, sure owners do it to their animals all the time. I think pets are happier in their own coats.

So there I was, naked. Except for a pink studded collar that Mandy just happened to have around. And eating on all fours off a plate on the floor. Well over to the side of the kitchen table where my Mistresses Veronica and Mandy sat, chatting like old friends over their breakfasts. I felt their eyes on me constantly, no doubt a benefit to me not eating where humans eat as my Mistress Veronica said. That I was easy to observe and damn if they didn't get a good show. Adhering to the rules of no hands meant some real challenges eating, constant direction changes. They both must've seen my exposed backside so many times. And it was one of these directional orientations where

91

I got the bright idea to try slurping up the food, creating a rather loud and obnoxious sound. I never saw it coming, swoo-SNAP!

"EYEEEEEE!!!"

Mistress Mandy said calmly with ice in her voice, "Manners, pet. We're not impressed with your vulgar sounds."

I glanced over my shoulder with a pout as she threw the twisted dish towel back over her shoulder and walked back to the table.

My Mistress Veronica said with a huge smile and glee I seen all over her face, "You are teaching me how to do that."

"Yes Ma'am, would be my pleasure and a necessary evil I suspect. This creature of yours may require a firm hand for her whole existence."

They both laughed as I went back to tonguing and lip pinching food into my mouth. Things had been going fine until that point. They had just elevated to really fine or even damn fine. I wasn't at all concerned I may start dripping arousal on the floor, I was so turned on. It took forever for me to get that plate cleaned but I managed. Throughout the task, it felt like I had eyes on all parts of me the whole time. I'm feeling so owned and I'm feeling so free!

"Oh pet! What is this?" Mandy asked in a frustrated tone while pointing at some egg white that had fallen on the floor and hidden under the edge of the plate. It became evident when she had taken the plate from me. "I worked hard on this food for you, that's not a good showing of appreciation. Tsk, Tsk!" What also became evident shortly after was my Mistress Veronica's natural talent with a towel or that she got excellent tips from Mistress Mandy.

swoo-SNAP!! "AAAGHHEEEE!

Damnation, that was good. Later some rubbing alcohol and a Bandaid was applied. My Mistress Veronica was very naturally skilled with a dish towel indeed.

Later I had fully dressed, ready to go out and feeling a little resentful. Of two things, the evil I had trespassed into meant needing to be prepared for certain threats when I wouldn't be ready to encounter them. The second was that we had to shift to normal and I had to get dressed. It really galled me that we couldn't be three adults who could get busy with all sorts of perversion, depravity and anguish without the concern of said threats interrupting that. Well me, My Mistresses Veronica and Mandy would be the deliverers of said torments. My preferences for them would be happy in their work and comfortable in making me uncomfortable!

Stupid bad people, making our lives difficult with their petulant and devolved shenanigans. My Veronica's voice was a blissful interruption of me and mine's usual cranial BS activities.

"What's wrong? You look, frustrated."

I turned and without saying a word just leaned into her, pressing my head against her chest. She put an arm around me, sensually placed her hand on where my head and neck met.

"Just thinking about what we have to think about before we can have serious fun with minimal worry. My only frustration is with the douchebags of the world thinking they're in the right to act so wrong."

"Oh, okay. I was just a little concerned we went too far in the kitchen. Mandy was also."

"Nope, my only problem with our kitchen activities were how you both seemed to half-ass things, maybe we all go to a pro dominatrix one day. She could teach you how to be better at your endeavours, heck, maybe you would pick up enough that I wouldn't need to trade you in!" I backed off at the last bit and blocked a playful yet well-formed punch. As if coming right from the block with a punch of my own inside her defences and then right to her cheek. But with my fingers and thumb in a pinch and a little jiggle of her pinched cheek the way grandmas do to their young-lings. Accompanied with an, "Oh, you little cutie!" Turned and walked out the door.

Veronica called after me, "I'm gonna hurt you so bad."

"With my help, right!" Mandy was already outside smoking a cigarette and waiting.

"Of course, in appreciation of your fine hospitality, my slave is yours to play with."

They both turned to look to Colleen. Only to find her back to them leaning on a fence. Her body language that of a person looking on in awe.

"You're a little dyke gear-head, aren't cha!" Mandy called to Colleen.

She replied with a shrug and said, "1968 Plymouth Barracuda Super Stock Hemi. She a stick shift?"

Mandy playfully replied, "What is it with you Cuda fans? They're some of the ugliest cars if not the ugliest of the muscle era."

Veronica piped in, "Totally, even if it's a Dodge thing, how about the Challenger, Dart, Superbee or even a Boss. All those other choices but you'd rather eye molest that ugly iron? Colleen turned around with a genuine look of upset on her face, instantly stopping any more heckling from the two.

"You shouldn't say such things about the nice old girl! She can hear you!" Which got Veronica and Mandy howling with laughter.

Mandy walked over to a gate, unlatched it, swung it open and dangled a set of keys in front of Colleen. "Go on then, go over and console her.

I smiled as I snatched the keys. Hollering over my shoulder. "There aught to be a hot line to call for reporting abusers like you two!"

Again the two women laughed and looked to each other shaking their heads. Then they walked over to join Colleen and her new friend.

After walking all around the ride and dropping to push up position at all four corners glancing underneath, Colleen pulled the hood lock pins and went over to unlock the drivers door. Mandy slipped in, then reached under the seat to pop the hood.

The three women stood in front of the fully dressed 426 Hemi, at which point no kindnesses or cruelties were uttered. Just silent respect was offered. "She's beautiful." Colleen said, handing the keys back to Mandy.

Mandy stepped back and shook her head no. "I owe you my life Colleen, go wind her out and let her feel some wind in her grill."

"That's not necessary Mandy, besides, technically we brought the trouble to you."

"Maybe so but you didn't leave me hanging in that hallway when you could have. I see my son again, it's largely in part thanks to you, thanks to you both. Heck, you may even get some knocked off the purchase price if you wanted to buy her. As my thank you."

Colleen just nodded and smiled, then she pulled her sleeve down over her hand and pulled the dipstick to check the oil. Satisfied with that, she checked other fluid levels and then with a caress of the hood brought it down to first latch and double palm, pushed it closed.

Item number thirty two on my list of buckets. She'd had plenty of opportunities behind the wheel of Detroit classics. A few even with an owner's blessing. But, never her favourite. Until now. After making sure all mirrors were adjusted, seat slammed fully forward she pushed in the clutch, turned the key and the motor caught. She felt the powerful motor's growling vibration, a caged up rage spilling into all parts of her flesh in contact with the car's components.

More than that, I feel it in my very being. In another life, I would've been a getaway dr...

"Would you three like some time alone?" Veronica groaned from the front seat in an aggravated tone, rolling her eyes and throwing her head back looking up at the headliner.

Mandy had a quizzical look on her face from the back seat.

Colleen, as if ignoring it all, stroked the wheel from twelve to to one to eleven and back to twelve while saying in the cheesiest endearing talk she could muster, "Shhh now, it's okay baby, just tune her out, pretend that mean little girl isn't even here." Then before anyone had a chance to express more vituperations, she aggressively grasped the pistol grip shifter.

Kicking the clutch to the floor board with the perfect force, slipped into first with it being welcomed home and gave her three bitches a start. The third of course being the car. The two girls were asses and elbows for getting situated being taken totally by surprise with the car lurching forward and them being given the tiniest hint of the monstrous power still in reserve. Being that the car was parked in the back yard, it was one of Colleen's proudest operator moments in her life. A fully charged golf cart with the accelerator floored would have caused more chaffing to the lawn. As Colleen tortuously crawled the Cuda through the large swing gate Mandy had opened, Mandy spoke.

"Damn, I hate you right now." grumped Mandy, "I have a hard time taking off on pavement with this thing and you do a perfect start on turf!"

"Maybe that's just because you suck at it." Colleen seethed with eroticism in her voice.

"Wow, she really does desire to draw the worst out of her owners." Mandy retorted to Veronica.

"Yes, I'm beginning to think that even with us whipping her to death, in her last moments she'd still be in need of more reforming."

This drew a barking laugh out of Colleen as she was maneuvering the car the last few feet of the driveway. As she looked left and right and was about to turn out, Mandy threw down the challenge.

"Go on, show us what ugly muscle can do."

Colleen did a quick sweeping glance of her passengers, both had put on the racing style restraint harnesses. "Okay," she said. She eased out onto the street and stopped, with the whole block to play with. No kids out in the yards, no pets visible and out wandering around. "Imagine there's a twenty on the dash, bet you can't even reach for it until I let off the gas."

Both women started to lean forward when the look of strain on their face showed their core strength faltering. They both were forced backwards into their seats at the half point on the block. Colleen brought the car back to sensible right before the stop sign. With suspension still rocking, Colleen squeaked, "1, 2, 3," and accelerated into the turn. With force enough to make everyone bobble head to the right to the slightest chirp of the tires. Colleen had the rear tires at their utmost limit of operation with out full differential lock up and breaking loose.

"I really, really hate you right now," Mandy growled.

"Firstly, I want you to bottle all that hate up, let it fester and then take it out on my hide later. Secondly, there's no measure of practice that can be defined as too much, you think I wasn't all jerky'lurch'y the first time I drove some serious power with standard and rear wheel drive." After a few seconds of no one saying anything, Colleen added. "Because you'd be correct, I was perfectly adept from the first."

"BAAA!" And "AHAA," groans of annoyance bellowed in unison from the passenger and back seats in such perfect timing, it was harmony. They all broke out in laughter that the car seemed to join in on as Colleen power-shifted to second on a main drag. She let off a second later when the speedometer showed well over the legal limit.

"This is torture," Colleen sighed.

"What?" Veronica asked, "That you two have to part ways at some point? Because you are not leaving me for a car! I'd hunt you down!"

Mandy promised, "If she did, I'll help you track her down, kill her and dig the hole!"

Colleen chuckles, "You bitches be awesome. No, driving this car in a world of laws, order and rules. Let alone in a city, I believe I'm doing her horrible wrongs whenever I have to ease up on the speed." Then it occurred to me before it escaped the dialogue of my mind, that it was the first time out loud saying"My Veronica" the first time said for my Veronica to hear.

"My Veronica, if I owned every one of these that ever came off the line, had to wreck 'em all... also knowing repairs to be impossible as well as none ever being built again." I removed my hand from the shifter, found my Veronica's and then placed hers around the grip of the shifter with mine coiled around both. Then dropped to first for a corner, came into it, burped the gas, as the rear end broke loose, the tires screamed in joyful torment. I finished with, "I'd melt 'em all down to buy you and I one more second of together."

In my peripheral, Veronica turned away, an index finger dabbing under her eye ever so discretely. Mandy stayed selflessly quiet in the back seat, striving to be nonexistent for the moment.

***

Colleen had a cart that was loaded up with all the essentials, as well as some wants... hardware stores were her toy stores. She was flush up again, pocket-cash wise. Both men at the hotel had neat folded wads that were around two grand each. Colleen didn't consider the money she had received from Veronica to be hers. Veronica had wanted to entrust her with a portion of the cash she and Colleen had taken great risk to acquire from her safety deposit box. Colleen had seen her logic on both of them carrying some of it.

She was so engrossed in the hardware store zone that she literally bumped her cart into Veronica's basket cornering to the next aisle. Colleen smirked, knowing what she would do next. First talk with her and then flirt with her as if she were actually a stranger that she really did just bump into.

Pouring on a thick Celtic accent, "Oh, my, sorry to crash ya like that, dear!"

The whimsical look that came over Veronica's face delighted Colleen.

"But seeing as fate has us colliding like this, my goodness, I'm glad of it."

Veronica was blushing, a beautiful orange skin tone, turning to red faster than the Cuda could wind out.

"You are as divine as a view of the rising sun over shamrock country; has anyone ever told you that?"

Looking left and right, ultra embarrassed, she mouthed, "You are dead, you are so dead."

"Oh now lass, you needn't deny it or worry on it, being a gift to any on this earth with eyesight is a gift you can give to all who… Okay, I'll stop." Colleen finished in her normal voice.

Veronica had started to look genuinely pissed, even though she had a smile trying to dig out of her mouth like a trapped coal miner.

Colleen suddenly suspected this lady never showed who she actually was when under the watchful eyes of the public, maybe when under any other eyes period. Colleen just assumed in the empty bar that when they were the way they were, it was all good. I'll converse with her later that when we are out, it'll be how she prefers, in whatever way she prefers.

Steering her cart around Veronica, she stopped when parallel and whispered, "Sorry, I truly would rather not upset you unknowingly like this."

Veronica whispered back, "It's okay, we'll talk on it later.

Mandy came out of a near aisle having seen the whispering and their smiles at each other and playfully spat out. "I hate you both." All three of them smirked.

Then I noticed both Veronica and Mandy eyeing up the cart, heaping with merchandise. "At the generosity of the fallen, plan on leaving most of this plunder with you when we part ways, hope you're okay with that."

Mandy just smiled and nodded.

Veronica looked at me with admiration on her face, a shimmer of pride swimming in her eyes.

Later, in the parking lot, Colleen asked Mandy if there was a long way back that offered higher speed limits for her to wind the Cuda out. Both ladies grinned which Colleen read as thrilled and excited grins.

When they had the last light before a freeway it was perfect. Through the intersection and fifty feet later was the freeway's posted limit sign. Also perfect was not a car around while waiting for the green. All of them being able to see the other light change to amber and then red. The ardour in the car seemed of measurable quantity. Roll the window down if it got to high in concentration.

GREEN.

Colleen had zero wheel spin and the pedal 3/4 to the floor, a quick test of the wheel revealed the front end was light. Still on the pavement but light, you can feel the difference in steering and body sway. Her passengers were all about the experience, hooting, hollering.

Veronica with her, "Oh ya baby!"

Mandy joining in with a, "Whoa snap!

Colleen was having the time of her life, driving her top-of-the-list dream car, two beautiful dames along for the ride and knowing what lay in store for her at their shared destination. I'm gonna have to give Mr Adams kudos, she thought, he was a tarnished and bent fork in the road I'm so glad I took. Everyone has at least one redeeming quality.

With nothing in the rear view the whole way back, Colleen gave her report when they parked in the yard. She had parked the Cuda on the lawn to give the grass some moisture and hand wash it the same time.

"The way I see this, we would have been in trouble by now if there was going to be any. Mandy, I think you're completely in the clear. I know that the authorities would have been knocking at your door or waiting out for you when we got back. If the authorities can't tie you to the events at the hotel then the bad guys shouldn't be able to either. Also, the bad guys would have showed at your place last night being as that's the usual time for the vermin of the world to be active."

The girls seemed at ease with that and there was a tangible feeling of comfortable as they unloaded the trunk. Having also stopped at a grocers, there were several trips into and out of the house.

"What did you have in mind for those?" Mandy asked as she was eyeing up the 2"x2" steel tubing lengths that Colleen carried into the house.

"Peace of mind for me when you two have me in any forms of strict and inescapable bondage," was her matter of fact reply. It had come up in conversation that Mandy's talk of chaining up Veronica and Colleen in the basement was idle. Though it was the incapability to do so, not the lack of desire that made it latent.

Colleen explained to Mandy that if she didn't want drop bars for security for the largest basement room door as a permanent fixture, Colleen would fill the holes she made and touch up the moulding paint before Veronica and herself pushed off. Mandy also seemed receptive of the benefit of a poor person's panic room if needed.

"It being the laundry room, you have water and access to sewage, stock it with some canned food, you could hold out for weeks." Colleen had stated rather normally.

Later on Veronica and Mandy were relaxing. Colleen had also purchased tools and was multi tasking between making some skill saw cuts and working the barbecue.

"I think you should chain this one to your hip and never let her go," said Mandy, then adding, "The bitch can cook, run a saw and drive like Steve McQueen.

They both sat on comfortable patio furniture nursing drinks, enjoying the sun and watching Colleen running here and there, yet seeming in total order with her bustling.

Veronica nodded and smiled. "Actually I'm hoping that she wants myself at her hip and won't ever want to let me go. If ever I knew her happiness only remained possible in her walking on, I couldn't keep her caged, chained or beholden to me in anyway. I think I'm coming to realize she's more of an untamed creature who wouldn't survive in the captivity of normal human civilization parameters."

"I hope I'm not overstepping here but, maybe that's why I'm so everything into her. Intrigued, attracted and etcetera."

"I know that's why I am, she's so special."

"So when you do release her back into the wild, can I live trap her in the hopes she'd survive my captivity, no hard feelings?" Mandy asked jokingly.

Veronica glare-smirked and flicked moisture off her drink's straw at Mandy. They both laughed.

"Are you beauties talking about me over here?" Colleen asked as she approached.

Veronica and Mandy cast glances at each other and looked back at Colleen.

"Just planning your demise, bitch." Veronica purred with a sinister smirk.

Mandy chimed in, "It's going to be brutal. We could be getting ourselves on an amnesty international list."

"Well that's nice to hear, here I'm sweating and toiling with all I do, hate to think you two are just filling your skin with meat as far as being productive goes."

They both looked at me with smiles more devious than I'd seen yet, if I could melt with anticipation of divine torments, I'd be a patio puddle.

By the time they were sitting down for beer can chicken and assorted veggies that had simmered in foil with a full package of bacon, Colleen was satisfied with fortifications.

"Oh my!" called out Mandy after her first few bites.

Veronica gasped. "It's like tasting paradise, Colleen. This is it. I now know what paradise tastes like!"

Colleen made a mock bow in her chair and felt a bite in her pants pocket, she dug in and looked a bit embarrassed. "Oops. I guess I kinda held onto these." I reached out, handing the keys back to Mandy.

Taking them, Mandy replied. "Sal good, I kinda thought you were committing to taking her off my hands. You do know, I think the three of you belong together." She finished, winking at Veronica.

Veronica smiled and asked. "What are you hoping to get for her?"

10

He heard enough over the phone to consider it warranted and was now in his car, en-route to the helipad. His shoulder holsters and eight pounds of the comforting burden they transferred to his powerful shoulders did little to improve his mood. It was a good feeling, being on a hunt and ready for taking of life. It just wasn't good enough. When things were balanced, he may look on it again as his last good operational violence.

The men in the car with him let seep from them their unease. He had a reputation. Even those under him that weren't yet born knew of the past when Sellkritch had been his most bloody. That felt good as well. Divers in a cage, in the same water he swam in, knowing the unease they felt. An aged evolved predator, in the same surroundings that you occupy. Can't fathom my decision now, that I made the choice to leave all this behind.

"Ten minutes till we are airborne, sir." The front seat passenger called back.

Sellkritch did not reply with more than a nod. His thoughts were of an era when all the world was filled with his kind. Half of it anyway, the other half were the nutrition.

In the helicopter, he got his next hourly from Sands. At a large expense the passenger cabin was near silent and the phone call sounded like it was from a busy library by comparison.

"Sir, there's been a development. Not in our favour."

"Explain!" He replied hostilely at the expense of his travel companions. He no longer cared about his influence over them.

"There is another interested party. The officer in charge of the hotel incident was good enough to call me concerning some men snooping around."

"Can we identify the other party?"

"No sir, they were long gone. However it seems we are still reputable in Wendasque's opinion. She shared a description because of her concern that the girl may be at risk."

"Her current level of involvement?"

"Limited, she has to play by the rules. She couldn't take action because of a bad feeling."

"But we can. Sands, you know this could mean an internal threat."

"Yes sir, that would be my assessment."

Sellkritch was quiet, mulling it over until he finally spoke. "We still have no objective that comes before the task at hand. Even if this is an indication of an internal power struggle, or more than an indication in the end. They may know the sway of power that could occur if and when they find her first."

"I'm of that opinion as well sir. We have all teams converging on the area. If it gets chaotic, and I'm thinking it will, the pell-mell that ensues is going to be here."

Dammit Sands, dial back the thea-pain-in-my-sarus. "It will, Sands. I'll be at your location in..."

One of the men in the cabin patched in to the pilot when he seen Sellkritch look the question at him.

The man held up one finger, then another hand representation that indicated, "less than."

"One hour or less, Sands."

"Yes sir, one team will be scouring close, and abort in time for your, pick up."

"Good. Twenty minute intervals for reporting, Sands."

"Yes sir."

Sellkritch scowled at the cabin of the helicopter. Blaming it for being the slower model. As if it was to blame for him not spending the extra few million. It's going to be a long 19 minutes, maybe too long.

Then Sellkritch smiled, there was only one complaint he ever had about hourglass Sands. When the pressure was on and or building, his intellect started to show in full. The man started thinking more, or was it that he started refraining less from his usual restraint. The man was gifted, to an extent he could make those around him feel inferior. So he would deliberately dial it back, until he blended with those around him. Sands was everyone and everything soluble.

11

Mandy was a little hesitant to reply but eventually got around to it. "I have looked at some comparable cars for selling prices and they go for quite a bit. I also have dreams of it putting my son through a year or two of college. And apparently it's blue book stock, with the exception of the motor and the super stock body dressing. All work done to the same specs as Hurst did with their run of the super stock, with all paperwork and history."

"My ex said his father wanted a sleeper, one that he could drive on the streets. Telling people she just looked fast, a tame little sheep in wolf's clothing. He even disabled the hood release and reconnected it to another hidden under the seat. Boys and their toys. He went so far as having saved the original tires and rims from show room and hung em in his garage. I'm getting them this fall."

Colleen interjected, "You should be asking no less than 80k. Hell, I'm guessing that crate 426 fully dressed is worth 10-12k by itself. If everything is as you say, she would easily sell with some heckling for 75. I'm holding out hopes for a neglected rust bucket in some farmer's garage one day. Mandy, you'll get fair market value, it just won't be outa my pockets. They ain't monie'd enough."

"Well, I did say I'd sell it to you for a reduced price. What could you see viable for yourself?"

"Mandy, no. Get top dollar for it and bank it as you planned for your son."

"You saved my life and even just this morning, the both of you have shared with me a lot. Making for one of the best days of my life."

Veronica stepped in with the perfect sentiment in Colleen's mind.

"We are all three of us are not one bit indebted to any in our little group, except continuing to be decent to each other as we have been."

"Ya, what she said." Colleen seconded with a pointed index finger from her beer hand, the other three and her thumb still clutched the bottle. "Besides, I've always seen it that the universe lays it out for us to play it out. Driving a super stock has always been a bucket of mine on the list, I can cross that off thanks to you. If I'm ever meant to own one one day, it'll happen and I'll feel right about the how. Not because of any feelings of indebtedness someone may have. If you really want to pay us back, amp up the cruelty the next time I'm naked."

All three of them broke into laughter that pushed any awkwardness out of the yard. They sat in the sun and felt its rays warming their bodies.

With Mandy on her days off from the bar and her son not being back for another week, it was decided Veronica and Colleen would forgo getting off to parts unknown. And, as of yet, parts undecided.

I collected up dishes, commenced to cleaning up after my projects, both construction and culinary related. Then left my two lovelies in the sun to talk. About my future torments I hoped.

"So she really has no hard limits? Mandy asked with surprise and some excitement in her voice.

"Ya, that's what she's led me to believe but, let me ask you a question. Ex, having a son and whatever else has been in your past, have you been with another woman before?"

Mandy shuffled in her chair. "I have only the knowledge that I am interested in women and kink play for the first time, which was thanks to you and your gal there.

Veronica nodded, "I, myself, knew since I was young, but because I was concerned about it not being okay with my family, I've never been with a woman either."

They both seemed to console each other with their mutual silence for a time.

"Look, I am totally aware you both have some pretty strong feelings for each other and I want some kind of assurance that I won't overstep in any way. Maybe we set some boundaries, anything you may not be okay with and all that."

"Actually Mandy, I think for the time we have to share, and I suspect what Colleen would prefer, the three of us say the hell with boundaries. Let's just move into these uncharted waters together, we'll see fair sailing and stormy seas but we'll be a communicative crew and adjust accordingly. I don't know about Colleen and her previous endeavours, I'm near certain she's had them. Though I do know that I'm happy to share my first experiences with you both."

Mandy smiled, "We are going to hurt her so good."

"Yes, yes we are," Veronica replied while they clinked glasses, then added, "though I think our little freak would prefer we hurt her so bad."

Some times the universe has crazy harmony, as it was with this time.

"And that works too," was what they both said simultaneously.

I heard the tremendous laughter from where I was in the house and hoped all the more. Hope that it's filled with glee about their future wrongs committed on me. I shivered with the goose-bumped flesh caused by a fellow traveller passing over my final destination, wherever that may be. Then smiled as I carried on with my work.

Forty-five minutes later I was just putting the last dish in the rack to air dry. Then I turned around to see a most wonderful sight and my jaw dropped. These two women standing at the entry way to the kitchen were dressed to kill. Their make up was super aggressive for style. They looked mean.

Veronica wore a pair of wet-look pants, maybe loose enough they were borrowed, some mean looking boots with blocky heels, leather bustier and a dominatrix cap.

Mandy had a look of her own, black cocktail dress, over knee highs with at least a three and a half inch heel. And was wearing black velvet looking opera gloves.

"Strip, bitch!" Veronica barked.

"Right now!" Mandy berated.

Oh gosh, I'm at the threshold to paradise, but I'm outside, looking in and hoping these Goddesses allow me admittance. I thought as I undressed, my eyes on the floor.

"That took too long, we'll make you pay for that later. You're not wearing heels Colleen, you need to crawl to us." Veronica chastised, promised, then stated and outlined.

"Oh look at her, she is so in need of our everything we will do to her, for her own good, can't even crawl well can you slut!"

"Permission to speak, Mistresses Veronica and Mandy?"

"Granted."

"Granted."

"Your slave can do better. Your slave will do better. Thank you Mistresses Veronica and Mandy." I finished, just as I had arrived a respectful distance from my two Goddesses. Close enough to be kicked, it seemed logical for present circumstances. Correction, it seemed logical for the present blissful circumstances.

"Sit back, slave, on your feet and knees, spread and present for your Mistresses." ordered Veronica

I snapped back and spread my knees out wide, fully exposed and presented before them both. Head and gaze looking down, not presuming myself worthy to admire them. Again, logical.

Veronica reached out with one of the heels that I had purchased and hooked the stiletto tip under my chin. As she applied pressure she spoke. "Look at us, slave."

I slowly raised my head, both women looking so incredible when above and looking down on me. I was revving up with arousal and the only contact to my physical form was the heel tip from the pump currently digging in under my chin.

"Listen and learn, slave, firstly, twice now you have put my name before Mandy's. From now on you will regard us as equals and every other time you will put one of our names before the other. Final warning, slave. Secondly, Mistresses Veronica and Mandy?" Veronica trailed off, for Mandy to finish.

"Slave, both of us deserve our proper title. No more of this Mistresses plural shit. If the minimal amount of talking we expect and condone is so much for you," She moved in and grabbed a hand full of hair at my scalp. "that you'll attempt to half-ass it with these disrespectful short cuts, what, to save your voice? We will put down a dish of water for our little bitch." She finished with a yank.

Shit, these beauties have brainstormed on this. I'm in trouble, Colleen thought. A sensuous, bounteous, wondrous trouble I can wrap around and cocoon myself in and never wish to emerge from.

"Do we have an understanding, slave?" they both asked in concert.

I'm in real trouble. Sweet, delicious and delightsome trouble. "Yes Mistress Mandy, yes Mistress Veronica."

"We better, slut. Now, we would like a report of the work you have done. Put these on and then you are permitted to stand."

After donning the pumps, I stood on shaky legs. More the excitement than being unsteady in the heels.

"Before your report," Mandy stated firmly, "You will in a ladylike manner, walk to that chair and bend over putting your hands on the seat, now!"

"Yes Mistress Mandy." Challenge time, I had never connected myself and ladylike in any of my self-made connections and associations. I had been honest and received pointers in the dress shop on posture and movement. Hopefully enough to please my owners and just shy enough that they still have criticism leeway. I swung and swayed and tried for some muscle flex in my movements for cake topping. Having arrived at the ordered destination, I assumed the demanded position.

"Walks more like a hooker than a refined lady."

"Agreed. In this town, I'm sure there are more than enough angry lesbians. So many, that pimping her out for endless debauchery and torment would assure a comfortable lifestyle for the both of us."

Good grief, I might cum right now, bent over this chair...

The sounds of impending peril, in the form of aggressive footwear marching toward me. Their wearers, vicious soldiers, always ready for the war on the inadequacies of a submissive. A war I would make necessary, prolong and could be found tremendously guilty of the crime of war profiteering.

"Sister, I bet I know something evidentiary of our little sub here being well suited to being our little whore."

"And I bet I know something of her still needing so much more correction. But, please sister, share with me," Veronica finished with a friendly tone.

"Well..." "SMACK!!!" With no warning, Mandy had slapped my right ass cheek with her satin-gloved left hand, her finger tips had actually landed on top of my exposed vulva. An even more painful sting.

I kept silent. Only logical.

Again with little to no warning, Mandy's gloved fingers plunged into my warm wet and waiting depths. The satin encapsulated fingers felt smooth and luxurious.

"Mmmmaa" I moaned in pleasure. Piss off logic.

SMACK!

"AAAHHHA!!! I cried out.

Mandy's right hand had found the side of Colleen's right breast hanging vulnerable. Found it with such force, it became a cue ball that slammed the left breast turned eight ball with force enough for a five point bank into corner pocket.

"We decide when your pleasure is permissible, bitch!" Mandy berated.

Ouch! I'm sorry. Logic, please come back.

Mandy pulled away her hand. Her glove fingers glistening with Colleen's excretions. "We've done nothing so far and the whore is ready to welcome a Soviet submarine up her snatch."

"Mmm, I see," Veronica's tone seething arousal.

Colleen had searched in vain for a reflective surface. In hopes of seeing her Veronica's face and that her face was at least showing acceptability of all this. Colleen would have deprived herself this nightmarish dream, the terror of which she could die happily in – if it was in any way not okay with her goddess. Hearing her voice, Colleen was assured she could assume the face matched. An audible showing of arousal that couldn't be masked with the entire stock of every fabric store in the world.

Mandy took her glistening fingers to Colleen's face with a measure of aggression, placing them above mouth and under her nose. Then painted a shimmering moustache of Colleen's juices.

Finishing with her fingers pointing upwards in front of Colleen's mouth.

"Permission to speak, Mistress Veronica and Mistress Mandy?"

"Granted."

"Permitted."

"May I clean your gloved fingers of my filth, Mistress Mandy?"

"You may, but be ladylike about it."

Just as my lips devoured Mandy's fingers, new fingers found their way inside me.

"Permission to moan, Mistress Mandy and Mistress Veronica?" I spoke as intelligible as I could with three fingers near throat deep in my mouth.

"You may."

"You are allowed."

"Mmmhhhaaw!" I moaned, welcome back logic, I missed you! Don't unpack though, I could be kicking you to the curb at any..."Aah-hga!" I squealed with mouth full of fingers.

My Mistress Veronica had dug in deep and gouged a bit painfully into my inner flesh.
"Not very ladylike at all!"

"Mandy, we should stop wasting our time now with hoping for easy success with this slutty whore and just get to treating her as one. Show her that she should be careful what she asks for."

I was just finishing with Mandy's fingers and had sucked and swallowed with every drawing back of my head. Expecting to be reprimanded or worse even for the best job accomplishment possible in these circumstances. Please worse. On to my next set of fingers laden heavy with my arousal.

"Mistress Mandy, Mistress Veronica, may I speak?"

Both girls mock gasped and in voices that screamed satisfaction spliced with glee by some sick science of tone, said in unison. "You slipped up, Colleen!"

Crap! That sneered pronunciation of my name, said by two of the most wonderful dames on planet earth, had me giggling inside like I was infected with giddy. Shit, shit, shity shit'sheroo! I'm in for it now.

Mandy walked away towards the kitchen counter, singing the words. "It's beginning to look a lot like dish towel time! Sex toys in every whore!"

Veronica broke out laughing and Mandy joined in. My Veronica's hand was jostling all over she was laughing so hard, as I was attempting to adequately clean my juices off her fingers. She placed her other on the back of my neck. Her hand placement and the anticipation of dish towel hell arrival caused flow anew. As my newly developed arousal dripped from within me. And then my third cruel mistress, Mistress Logica, if she could, would have whispered in my ear. "You're screwed now, so totally and supremely screwed, enjoy!"

What a bitch.

Mandy had set up station behind me and I knew not why. Once situated, she took stock of my fully exposed rear. Then expressed her thoughts.

Who would have thought such pleasure, with the subtlety of a plane crash could be derived from such words of displeasure.

"Oh sister, do you see what your filthy, dirty, vile, little creature has done? I mean, if you weren't my best friend ever!"

Veronica spoke in the most apologetic of tones. "I know, she really is worthy of any cruelties we can only hope to invent, let alone those that already exist as well."

Mandy nearly broke the mood with what she said next. "I'm sorry, my bestie." Then gave Veronica a spontaneous hug as if to console. "It's not your fault. Unlike with dogs, simple creatures that they be, they simply can't be bad unless they are shown that's to be expected of them. That!" she said, pointing at me, should be able to be better, choosing so, no matter what she is shown."

Veronica nodded solemnly, perfectly playing the role of embarrassed owner as Mandy was walking away.

And towards me and if I wasn't the me that I am, the look she bared might be having me add to my mess of arousal with some urine a' la fear. It was the most beautiful of sinister smiles I thought possible.

She kept the look locked in, thank goodness, as she yanked one of the dish towels off her shoulder. Grabbing diagonal corners and giving it a one, two, three spin and landing it perfect under my chin. Drew it up tight and I felt the swell in my head.

That feeling a finger makes when the blood flow gets trapped with the petulant wrap of an elastic or string. Such a wonderful feeling, being choked by this delightfully depraved woman in a way that leads to death. I'm such a freak, such a grateful and appreciative freak. As I thought I heard Mistress Logica whisper, "Are we having fun yet sweetie?"

Mandy let off and the room was almost spinning. Thank goodness I'm bent over holding the seat of a chair. Only sensible, and sensible is all I have at this point. My Logica has abandoned her loyalties to me in favour of taking pleasure in my displeasure. Such a bitch.

My breathing pretty hard made it easy for Mandy to turn a garrote into a cleave gag. As she pulled it tight into my mouth, stretching my lips. She again played with ruining the mood with an apology.

"I'm sorry, I know I loose my temper at times. It just comes from a place of caring, I care for Veronica and I know how much she cares for you. You know it's really your fault, making this so hard." Which she coordinated with a pull deeper into my mouth. "We can fix you so you are worthy of kneeling before her and we'll keep at it."

In a voice only a gagged mouth can achieve, "Ys Mstis Mndy, Tnk yu Mstis Mndy."

She almost gently caressed my cheek, then pinched it hard and really jiggled it, "Oh my goodness," she had lowered her self to look me in the eye, "You with this gag, oh you little cutie!"

Gee, I wonder where that came from.

Swoo-SNAP! "KIIAAAEEGEEA!!!"

The dish towel must have been flying the nanosecond my cheek was released. Welcome to linen hell. Please clock in for your what'll seem like an eight-thousand-hour workday. Remember to desire to don the appropriate personal protective equipment that won't be provided even if it was available to protect your skin from physical impact fire. Have a wonderfully not nice day!

The next strike seemed to be a long time coming. I knew better than to turn around or stand up. Not out of fear of consequence, I could stop this whenever I wanted. I never wanted it to end. I had thought I heard them whisper and then some steps and the door open and close...

Then, what seemed like lifetimes of anticipation waiting, arrived.

swoo-SNAP!! "AAAAHHHHAAA!!!"

My Veronica clunked over, footfall only she could make sexy. Once she was off to the side where I could see her boots and those amazing legs. That pretty much being termination of view, I chose to stay frozen in position until told otherwise. Only sensible, funny really, the majority of my life I make choices that aren't. Majority of my decisions show the lack of sensibility that most of my gender possesses. But not now, I so much want to please my Mistresses, and want to continue coming up short in that endeavour.

"Look at me, slut."

I slowly raised and turned my head, trying to make my sightline's journey last as long as possible. Taking lifetimes to make that journey would still be sensible investments made. My Veronica, so lovely in all ways.

Our eyes met, I strived for the perfect blend of fear, happiness and appetite. In my eyes, my face, in every atom of my very being.

"You still need a lot of work, you know you do. At this point I'm still of the belief you are worthy of your Mistress's attentions." Veronica paused and re-twirled her dish towel for dramatic effect. She sensually reached under my chin, clasped firmly and raised my posture a tad higher. "I desire that you welcome Mistress Mandy back when she arrives."

"Ys Mstis Vewaniha."

"Ha!" She laughed once, "Your gag talk is so cute!"

"Tnk yu Mstis Vwaniha."

And on cue, Mandy returned to the kitchen.

"I am satisfied that her screams could be louder and we still have no concerns about this frustrating project of ours being a frustration for anyone else."

Oh, good. Yeesh! I can scream louder. And these two diabolical dames now know they can make me scream louder. Goody!

Then my two Goddesses started whispering, detail of the dialog between them was elusive. Then they both spoke together.

"You now know there are no limits, none. Not the pain we inflict, nor your responses to it, we own you now."

Their words were harmonious to me. In the perfect blending of their two voices, perfect timing of it and the message to me. Their slave. If it all ended here, if this was as far as my torment at their hands went, they still have me, near entirely. There would be a loyalty inside me to the both of them, a commitment nearly unbreakable. Save only by my own moral compass.

"Mstis Vewonka, Mistwis Mindy, phremisen tu pheek."

"Yes pet."

"Slave may."

"Yoer slve iphh gayphl phr yoi onrsip ober hur. Tnk ew."

12

On the city's outskirts, a large industrial park was quiet. All but one of the industrial properties were dormant, resting for another long day of industry marching on. The cement plant was on a temporary shutdown, all staff and management given time off with pay. Official correspondence and paperwork had been delivered, due to the age of the facility, an inspection and possible structural reinforcement would be ongoing for an undetermined period. Insurance companies and the related requirements can be demanding. Management would be kept informed and all staff were expected to remain on call. They were also quite glad and appreciative of the unknown amount of time off, no questions asked, no answers needed. This was one example of how some organizations operated. Creating circumstances of zero doubt and one hundred percent certainty, hidden and operating in plain sight. A chameleon's appearance of normal situations on the surface of its flesh, the deep tissue beneath, was where the unseen swaying of secret ripples took place.

Now, late at night, early, waiting just a short time away, the plant was home to industry of a different type, though it also was an industry that moved forward. A team that was eleven strong, its remaining nine, occupied the facility as a temporary base of operations. It met all requirements. Seclusion, secure, various pieces of machinery that could be employed to disappear a body. The remaining nine, after fourteen hours were fully set into their new surroundings, however, they had yet to settle. Every man was aware of the two operatives having been knocked off the board. The two men had been sent to capture a target, then deliver that target back to the site they now occupied. The two men never came back, never reported failure, and never would do anything ever again. The fallen never do.

Mortan had just finished berating one of his men. He had wanted to beat him to death. It may not have been the man's fault, but Mortan never cared about that. Even when there wasn't so much riding on it all, he never felt the need to show respect to a subordinate. They knew who his father was. Respect was what they owed, not what they were owed themselves. His father operated differently. He was soft, the old way of it.

If anyone can bring the organization together and to new heights in a new age, it's going to be me. He just had this integral piece to put in place and the other most powerful father of the organization would be out of the way. But right now that piece was in the wind. And while that was the case, no rest, no mercy, hell, he'd deny them food if he could. You don't succeed, you don't eat.

Mortan had yet to do it with one of his own, but he had starved a man to death. He had chained him to a cement floor and waited for him to die. His pride at how he dealt with it was short lived. His father was not pleased. "It's no way to dispatch an enemy, Mort," his father had chastised. Mortan knew his own rage was only a sign of his strength, indicative that he should lead and his father should step down. Or steps his father should be kicked down. Mortan smiled at the thought. The old man yelling out "Mort" one last time before his life was cut short.

Now he could only take solace in the idea of taking control of it all. His inept people were worthless, if he had an army of those like himself, he would rule it all. The hotel was their best chance, the men sent there had died. They didn't deserve as quick of a death as they got! Lucky for them they did. They would have been the first of my subordinates to be starved to death. Chained to that floor, day three or day four maybe, the same dish I would be eating would have been served before them and well out of reach.

I need to install cameras in that room, I can eat while watching their suffering when not able to devour the same dish. Then enjoy the video footage of it later. That's how I'm gonna get what I want from that bitch. Chain her up like a dog. You want food and I want compliance. She will comply. Mortan was lost in thought of his schemes when a man nervously approached. He was in better spirits being in his drug-spawned mental meanderings on the suffering of others. It was not to last.

13

Mortan had a cheery demeanour, as he liked to see those under his leadership uneasy. Those who serve should be fearful of those they serve. He gave a flippant hand motion for the man to report.

"We did what you asked at the hotel, got nowhere, we also have the impression that there may be knowledge of our presence here."

Mortan struck the man in the head, turned and walked away. Now he needed a fix like no one ever had.

When he had departed, two of the remaining men moved together. They conferred, quietly.

Romero and Dean had both been assigned to the heir to the throne, their discussion was not an easy one. "Dean, this is getting out of hand, we should contact his father."

Dean glared at him. "You know damn well that ain't the way we're gonna play this. If there is one person we can't protect Mortan's son from, that's himself. We take our chances that we are still alive when the dust settles. If Mortan ends up having dust settle on him, then we are all the better off. This is the life we were born into, Romero, and it's one we had every opportunity to step away from. We didn't have to follow in our fathers' paths, but we did. You make a choice, you stay the course of it. Or you didn't deserve to have a choice to make in the first place, it should have been made for you."

Romero whispered angrily, "Ya, all right but that junkie is gonna get us all killed. And when we're bleeding out next to each other, not one fuckin word. Only cheer I'll want then is the cheer I know I'll have. To know I ain't hearing any more of your philosophical bull shit." He walked off to light a cigarette.

Dean doubted the man could spell philosophical. But he wasn't dumb. Every day under Mortan's orders increased the percentages of no more days being the smart bet. The kid was a freight train at full power with every damn component rattling loose. The bad day Romero feared wasn't a possibility. It was the eventuality, just a matter of time.

He had knelt down to check for a pulse from the pile of meat on the ground. He was fiftyfifty on surprise of finding one and not. Mortan had a bad reputation for a lot of things, one of them being his near inhuman might. He may have held the record for punch force in the world. If there was such a thing. Mortan had killed a lot of men, his time in the organization. Three were in anger. One punch was all it had took.

Dean waved two men over. "See about waking him up, will you?"

One of them asked with his voice full of apprehension asked, "And if we can't?"

Dean smiled and said as he looked him dead in the eye, "Be about the same as him waking, not being able to add or subtract anymore. Wouldn't it?" The man nodded sombrely, turned, knelt down and began shaking the unconscious man by his shoulders. Dean added, as he walked away. "This is the life."

Dean went to light one of his own, and hated himself for it. What a fucking stereotype. Bad guys smoke, gimme a fuckin break. It wasn't to do with the health aspects, or the image either. It was the fuckin' money. And more principle of the thing than affordability, what he last heard about government taxation on tobacco products made him laugh. And I'm still hitting potholes with my Lexus because why? Dirtier than we are, fuckin crooks.

He found his charge, Mortan, sitting on a stack of tires, rubber tube still draped loosely over his arm. I'm responsible for this mess of the Mortan legacy. Dean thought. He leaned in against the wall and waited for him to become less suggestible then he was now. I could talk him into cutting his own wrists with plastic safety scissors right now. There's a thought...

Dean contemplated this as well as butting out his smoke before it was half way done. Just outa spite. Both idle contemplation's really. He knew he'd fill the time with several more continuously burned to the filter. Waiting for Mortan to come to enough, knowing he'll ask me. "Dean come over and talk with me. We need to strategize."

Then I'll do most of the talking, outlining prudent points, come up with multiple strategies and so on. He'll throw in the occasional, "That's sound judgment," and a lot more, "I don't know how I feel about that," and so forth. Then he'll reword one of my notions preceded with, "Now what you think about this one I've been working on?" Or maybe he'll OD, we can throw him in the car and all go home. That would work too. Damn I hate this fuckin job.

So, I may as well get in the game now, he pulled out his pack, ve-toed the decision and slammed it home angrily. If I was on the run, last sighted at a hotel, where would I be now. Another hotel? The fuck outa town? It doesn't do me any good kicking myself around in her life choices. It's doubtful she'd be the tactician that I am. Though that bit with the truck was clever, had us searching those woods for 15 min-utes before I ordered an all-stop.

Took me a while, but I discovered in our haste, the only tracks to and from the truck were ours. And she wasn't driving, according to a homeless man outside the bank, and our men sent there to bring her in. I still don't know why Mortan changed his mind and cancelled the contract. If he has ideas about forcing her to be what he wants? Dean put the notion out of his mind. Ignorance is bliss, he thought. Two years back, Dean's little sister was raped, he got the boss's blessing to handle it himself.

He had just lit a smoke and knew he'd be hard pressed to keep from killing his boss's first son if it came to the bastard doing what he's been known to do.....

"Dean, come talk with me, we need to strategize. Hey! You got an-other one of those for me?"

Here we go, Dean thought, as he walked over, pulling his pack. Like gears designed to mimic the only truth of it all, the passing of time. "Here you are, boss, I don't know why you always bring me in on these strategy sessions. You're always the one coming up with the best way to go."

"Who will I have at my side when I'm in charge, none of these numb nuts. I need to train you up for our future, Dean, my old pal."

Dean kept it from his face, hopefully also his eyes. But at this moment he thought the best way to go was to knock him over and tip all the stacks of tires on him. Poor gasoline over it all while the junkie prince still laughed, then set the lot a blaze. He sat down on a nearby pail instead and played his part as usual. Bide your time, Dean, bide it well. The right time will present itself.

14

"Mstwis Mndy, Mistwiss Vawanaka, mai Igh sceek agahn."

Mandy first spoke to Veronica, "Oh, don't you just adore her gag talk!"

"Right! I know! So cute!"

"Yes, slut."

"Whore may speak."

"Weckom bk Mstis Mundy, Ey msd ew. I mssd yor atensons Im nt wrdy of."

"Hmmm. You do surprise me at times slave, you may be worthy of them, of our attentions. Maybe worthy of kneeling before us. Though I don't know, was that your idea to welcome me back? Answer me truthfully slave."

"Nw Mstic Mndi, sut has Mistiss Vwonaca tu tnk fo dat."

Mandy turned to Veronica. "Thanks my dear for that warm sentiment, sent via our live, walking and talking not so well ho-marc card."

They both started up with laughter.

Then Mandy pulled into view a roll of duct tape. My eyes went wide with genuine concern. She placed the roll on the chair in between my thumbs as my palms were pressed to both sides and fingers wrapped around the edges to underneath.

"Time for our tour of defences and fortifications, Colleen!" Mandy commanded.

"We had better be impressed Colleen!" Veronica added.

The way they both sneered my name gave me inner warmth, like it was cruelty saying niceties. "Ys Mstws Vwanica, Yeth Mistewis Mindi. Mstwis Mndy, Mistws Vewnica, ma slve hv sm watta?"

"Yes slave but, you're going to have to earn it, debt paid later."

"Yes, we we're going to give you four more towel lashes from each of us added to the two you already received to make ten. Veronica added. Now you'll get thirteen, four each from both of us and three for the water."

My head sank, "Es Mistws Vewannca, ys Mistwis Mndy." Mostly to hide the excitement billboarded on my face. Eleven more lashes, to parts unknown. A few more to my ass is great but I hope they remember other sensitive areas. And the duct tape has me so excited. If arousal was flammable, were I ignited, I could propel the next NASA shuttle to the moon. Or burst in to a cataclysmic fireball on the launch pad. I'd like to think I'm well engineered though. We'll see if they know how to use that magical gray tape for inescapable bondage.

My two Mistresses placed four bags on the table, the two I had seen were from the hardware store. The two I hadn't, were from the adult toy store and contained wonderful torments, I'm sure. The bags had me as excited as an elephant seeing a full peanut sack. But there were also bags in the basement, some gifts for my Mistresses. Thinking on it may have been a mistake, I was self lubing up all over again. A glorious, glorious mistake with possibly wonderfully awful ramifications.

"Hey!" Mandy called out. You never mentioned what you knew that meant our work with this bitch may go on and on, maybe for ever." She remembered as she was grabbing a bottle of water from a cupboard. She then thought differently and put it back, closed the cupboard and placing her towel through the handle.

"Ah yes!" said Veronica as she pulled a pink pet water bowl from the one hardware store bag. Then holding it, she looked the question at Mandy.

"Over where pet had brekkie this morning."

After placing the bowl, Veronica approached me from behind as I looked down at that damn duct tape. She started at the knot in the towel. "I'll bet you the last lash that her honest answer on her thoughts at the time we spoke will illuminate it proficiently. Damn, we may need to cut this gag."

Mandy giggled her hand to her mouth, "Oops, no biggie. I have lots."

"Mistis Mnady, Mstwes Vawanca, ma I hep?"

They both conferred with shared looks.

"Yes slave."

"We will see if you can, slut."

I stood, feeling a darling stretch of muscles in my lower back. Then walked over to my pile of clothes where they were neatly folded. Easily located the multi-tool on the outer edge of the stack and removed it from the case. Upon standing I opened it to pliers mode and turned to walk back. Arriving in front of Veronica and Mandy with my head bowed, the multi tool laying in both palms, a sacred offering.

"Mstwiss Vewanaca, Mistwis Mandy, da pwyers wll hep wiph de noth."

"We will see if you can!" my Veronica snapped impatiently.

I nodded and dropped to my knees in the previously required position. Legs spread and on near full display. Seemed sensible.

"Good slut," she said.

"Mstwis Vawanaka, Mistwiss Mndy, mai Igh tun mi bac tu yu bot." Shit! Did I?

"Yes."

"You may."

Did they miss it?

"And you also may look forward to your 10 additional lashes for failure to adhering to the simple order of showing us equal respect."

Shit. Absolutely fantastic caca. As I turned around I gripped the pliers in dominant hand and swept hair over my shoulder with the other. Then finding the knot and applying some blind mechanizing. With both fingers and the needle nose pliers, I had the second stage knot loosened up in seconds.

"Nimble fingers, bitch," Mandy said as she took the multi tool away. "We'll be sure to keep that in mind with your future immobility."

Hmm... a challenge.

"Turn to face us, slave." She spoke again.

When I had turned, Mandy was simply pointing to the cupboard with the towel threaded through the handle. "Fetch."

I stayed down and made to crawl.

"You're in heels, slut, that means you walk!" Veronica barked.

I'm so twitterpated with all this! I slipped up on the equal billing! I forgot the walk or crawl rules! This is great! I can see where this was going. As I got to the cupboard I bent over and found both ends of the towel with my mouth. Clenched my teeth and opened it. The bottle was too low to be retrieved in my teeth bent over, especially in these heels. So I dropped to knees, balanced and prepared to acquire my prize. I swallowed before I clenched the bottle in my teeth, trying to keep saliva off the lid and used my head to close the door. Then got up and walked back, then resumed the position.

"You see!" Mandy exclaimed with clear discontent. "Your creature is very smart. It's obvious she chooses to be obstinate just to aggravate our calm demeanour." She moved her hand to clutch the bottle. "Release pet!"

I unclenched and the bottle dropped.

"It's obviously intentional she didn't return my towel at the same time she brought the water." Mandy stated to Veronica.

Expecting the impossible? Na, I'm pretty sure I coulda pulled it off. Still, unfair expectations, sexy. Very cruel and, sexy.

Veronica shook her head in the affirmative with the same look of embarrassment for her difficulties that Mandy had to share in. "Thank you Mandy, really, thank you for your patience with my inadequate property."

Yes, so sexy.

"Mandy placed her hand on Veronica's shoulder, but before saying anything to her,snapped her head back to pierce my very soul with her dissatisfied gaze. Then pointed in the direction and snapped. "Hello? Towel!"

"Yes, Mistress Mandy." I replied, then I rose, turned and walked to my objective as I heard Mandy again.

"I'm here for you in these trying times. We'll get through this, together. Or we keep her in constant bondage as a creature most untenable."

So, so, so… sexy.

As I turned back, Veronica and Mandy had taken seats at the table, leaving my leaning chair in between them. That's a trap. Such a wonderfully inviting trap. I just want to skip, prance and dance most happily into it. Next time! I returned with towel relatively centred in mouth, head bowed. Then stepped forward while sliding the chair in under the table and stepped back. Left on full display to my Goddesses.

"Your throat sounded quite dry slut. We'll moisten that up in other ways later on. Go have a little drinky and then return to us to explain to your Mistress Mandy and I how your mind works."

Trap number two. And I'm being ordered to walk into it.

"Yes, Mistress Veronica." Arriving at the water dish had me excited like this morning had. Only this time the prospect was drinking with no hands. If my vaginal secretions were judged again I would be just as screwed as the last check up. Hopefully, literally screwed.

Down on all fours, having nothing to go by I just lowered my chin into the dish. I was able to submerge my bottom lip but after three swallows that was ineffective. Tongue practice for future events? As I discovered, lapping up water with your tongue is hard work.

Homage to labradoodle's the world over. Not practice, work out for many future events? When the water dish was nearly empty my sight went to the bottle close by. Maybe a quarter to a third was poured in the dish. Around nine lashings to get the remaining hydration. Twelve if I'm lucky.

Upon returning to the table, I was ordered to kneel, legs spread on full display. And then ordered again.

"Slave, share your unique mind's inner workings with us," Veronica commanded.

"Yes, Mistress Veronica." I obeyed in verbatim. Giving them both the word-for-word narrative of my own thoughts as the neutrons firing had created them.

"Good grief, I might cum right now, bent over this chair... The sounds of impending peril, in the form of aggressive footwear marching toward me. Their wearers, vicious soldiers, always ready for the war on the inadequacies of a submissive. A war I would make necessary, prolong and could be found tremendously guilty of the crime of war profiteering..."

"And that was what you thought right after I said..." Mandy started, but never finished.

Because I interrupted, just to be frisky, with what she had said, again in perfect replication. Just to show off.

"Agreed, in this town I'm sure there are more than enough angry lesbians. So many, that pimping her out for endless debauchery and torment would assure a comfortable lifestyle for the both of us."

Mandy sat there looking at me for around 20 seconds and then pointed at me, turned to Veronica and playfuly yelled. "You see! It's all deliberate! All her shortfalls when she could and should be a perfect submissive but chooses to be difficult!"

Veronica had a smirk break free and tried to capture it with her hand over her mouth. Useless. laughter was contagious. It mutated, went airborne and we were all infected. We were our own laughing village.

After a while, we stopped and sat there. Well, they did, I knelt. Two gorgeously dolled out dominatrix and my naked self. I was comfortable in my own skin. As was I more than comfortable with being certain our strict domination play could fire back up from its freeze-framed pause at 11:53: and however the heck how many seconds.

Veronica and Mandy looked at each other and shared nods.

"Colleen," Mandy said with no heartfelt sneer to it. Grab a beer if you like and come tell us some more of your unique mental operations. But you stay naked though."

"Yes, our slave stays naked." Veronica concurred.

Colleen gave them a quick rundown of how she had triggered her access of facts accumulated throughout her life. "The retention was accomplished already, just a matter of the access." I explained. I speculated on how it may have been preceded by training myself to be aware of the time within a tenth of a minute.

Telling them how once when I was concussed, it was thrown to epically inaccurate proportions of plus/minus 5 minutes for a few days. "We look at clocks numerous times in a day, without realizing it we are resetting our internal clock accuracy every time we do." Which led into my mental alarm of either a set time, or triggering it to wake up to any specific sounds I program myself with just before sleep.

Mandy and Veronica looked on with warmth and awe in the facts I stated about myself. Facts that made me feel weird and an outsider from fellow members of my species. Yet I felt warmth and gratitude for their acceptance. It has always been the case that I wouldn't be embarrassed to ask a girl to spit on me but I would have died of shame if I had to talk about my adaptions induced by the requirements I placed on myself.

"So you think what? The next step in human evolution is just waiting for the individual's demand of said evolution?" Mandy asked

"Maybe it's just more Darwinian than that, take any organism of any size and definitions of complexity. Take it from its known environment, drop it into a new one and 99.9 percent of the time you'll observe adaptation or the attempt to do so. It's a survival thing and point one percent is probably a gross over-calculation of the times where a creature chooses to roll over and die."

"A lot of what I'm capable of, if not all of it, is often found in military training and what is the military in regards to a soldier. Just a new and different environment, the soldier is the organism and the successful training is really the choice made. Or not. Trained soldiers are just a new version of themselves. The adapted version, an organism now more prepared to be dropped into many other different unknown environments. More capable of future adaptions to ensure survival."

Veronica was intrigued, "So to say people can't change is a falsehood. Drop a lazy person on an island where survival means they can't afford to be lazy any more and the change should be imminent."

"For the most part, I would say yes. I feel I should point out that I never went to university and chose the field of study for all this. I just observe and hypothesize."

"Like Einstein." Mandy stated, "Veronica, your pet is a genius."

"Our pet." Veronica corrected.

Mandy smiled back somewhat sheepishly, obviously hesitant to traipse down that road with more emotional landmines than was needed to take someone's legs out from under them.

Colleen was about to go way over her skis, then stopped herself.

As if she noticed, Veronica asked her. "Something to add, pet?"

"Yeah, and I hope it's okay with you."

"I trust it's always going to be the case with you, that logic and simple sensibility will be a prevalent factor in anything you'll say, or do. So in my mind, it's guaranteed to be okay."

"Well, okay then. Mandy, I believe you are concerned with what we have going on here and where it may be going. Good for you, that's your very capable inner organism evaluating a new environment. And guess what, My Veronica, I believe is in no lesser or greater a predicament. And then there is myself, which I can guarantee both of you lovelies that's exactly where I am. As well as that environment can be defined. Different from any other I've chosen to delve into. We three of us know very little about each other at this point, not nearly enough to make any decisions on anything of any major importance."

Veronica looked on towards Colleen, at her, into her and through her. Seeing a human being that may be truly pure, because of that animalistic side of herself. By her own explanation, an adaption on her part due to environments she dropped into by choice. Veronica felt grateful for all the turmoil that had led to her life having been forfeit. Grateful for the organism Colleen had morphed into, knowing she was alive because that organism had chosen to be adaptable.

Mandy spoke, bringing both Veronica and Colleen out of yet another one of their sessions of staring into each others eyes and smiling with each other.

"Hell with it, maybe we can just promise each other this one chosen success of our adaptation as our new environment becomes known. Or even if it is an adaptation that will succeed by a sheer force of nature. That our friendship remains or adapts to that which is even more."

"Our friendship, a highly adaptable organism. Choosing for itself or us choosing for it to adapt for its survival." Colleen stated before she finished the last of her beer.

Veronica added, "To Darwin, one smart bird watcher." She also thought that it was an unquestionable truth. We three would have gone on living our lives being all the more empty inside; if it weren't for random events putting us on a new path we all walk down together for a time.

All three sat in silence, not an uncomfortable one but comfortable and contemplative.

Mandy broke the silence, "So Colleen, tell me. Is there a way to securely duct tape the chair you sit on to the floor?"

Veronica smiled, "Yes Colleen, teach us."

I quivered, some cosmic force hit 'play' on the remote.

After a quick walk through the house and a rundown of all possible means of entry, multiple scenarios and how best to react, the three of them were back in the kitchen. Colleen was tearing multiple strips of duct tape off the roll, while reflecting on the tour she gave. Colleen had explained to Mandy that all striker and deadbolt plates had been given longer screws. She had set beer bottles on all three door knobs for an early warning. Strips of wood, painted to match the window casings, were in all window tracks. As she had given the tour of fortifications, naked, wearing only her white high heels. It was strange.

A perfect blend of the two opposing forces of myself. My inner warrior and my chosen submissive in harmony with each other. Unlike their normal being at war with each other. I am really glad that I hitched that ride with one of my fellow sociopaths.

Both Mandy and Veronica were amping up their inner dominatrix with berating and criticisms.

"Work faster, slave!"

"This is taking too long, slut."

"Mistress Mandy, Mistress Veronica, slutslave is trying to do a good job, as efficiently as she can."

"I don't know about you, Mandy, but, I'm getting tired of hearing her excuses and back-talk." Veronica had been twirling up my dish towel and walking around behind me as she spoke.

"Yes, thank you Veronica, I've had enough of this slave's talking."

Mandy bent down, reached in and tightly clamped down fingers and thumbs on both of my nipples.

"Aaagh!" I squealed, mouth wide open, the perfect open, an open invitation. For the twisted towel that swung with no fault at all right in deep up against the beginning of my lips. I could feel the dampness of the cloth as if somehow it was marked territory. That towel belonged to my mouth and my mouth belonged around it. If there was any doubt on that, it would be washed away by my inner juices that were developing anew.

"More hard work before us, Mandy."

My Veronica spoke as she tied off the towel behind my neck. Perhaps a bit tighter than Mandy had tied it previous.

"I'm certain of that, hang on, I need to check something."

"Smack!"

"Phwaahh!"

Mandy must've had her hand resting on the floor just under my ideally exposed vulva. Sitting on my haunches in these damned wonderfully tight heels gave her about twelve inches for building some momentum. It not only lifted me up from my crouch an inch or so but hurt like hell. I love having my pussy slapped, who knew right? More un-foretold abuse ensued as her ring and middle finger plunged into me aggressively. They were not impeded in driving home in any way whatsoever. My internal moisture anew saw to that.

"Yes, as I feared."

She muttered just before starting to dig around inside me like an angry badger. The simple task of placing eight inches of duct tape on the floor, the remaining four inches of it travelling up the metal tubing of the chair leg was rocket science with my arousal going supernova.

She withdrew her fingers and showed Veronica the measurable volume on her gloved hand and fingers.

Veronica was just visible in my peripheral and that head shake hung low with the being ashamed of me on her face wasn't helping me slow down. What came next didn't help either. But it made me glad I found Mandy's mop earlier for giving the linoleum a once over.

"I think this is going to be necessary." Veronica stated while rummaging through one of my excitement bags on the table.

I kept going with my task, now having the first leg secured. Four strips of tape at the four quarters of analog clock, 3,6, 9 and 12 traversing the floor to chair leg. Four more strips travelling the floor perpendicular over the tape just before the chair leg. And then a final strip wrapping around the chair leg over all four of its strips. The quick test of how secure it felt also didn't help me slow down my Indy car of an impending orgasm.

Having just finished tearing the next nine strips of tape and placed them neatly dangling on the edge of the chair seat, I felt it and heard it. Oh no! Veronica had placed a vibrator on my exposed happy place! What I heard was the vibration of some kind of commercial ground tamper. What I felt wasn't heat, vibration or pain but all three coiled into some evil new hybrid super-snake of sensation!

I was glad I cleaned the floor because I was going to be squirting all over it. And I was glad because I was hoping my owners were going to have me lap it up.

"Mstwis Vwanka, Mistwes Mndy! Igh cnt hld bck, Im gewng tu cum!" I scream moaned around my cleave gag. My hair was aggressively clenched, my head pulled back. I was bracing and pulling on the chair, by some miracle diagonally opposite the leg secured. It held fast.

"These choices aren't up to you any more slut." Veronica whispered in my ear. "And you have to ask before you do."

I heard the clink of a dish placed on the floor but it hardly registered in my pre-planetary explosion of inner heat.

"MAI EY CUMM!!!!" I screamed around cruel twisted cotton.

Two voices and their accompanying breath in each of my ears were dual firing pins on my primer.

"Yes."
"Yes."

"AAAAAAGGGGHHHHHAAAA!!!"

And it felt like I shot hot lead from my vaginal barrel. So glad I asked permission to pee during the fortifications tour, or was I? The room was just coming back into focus, a hazy, blurry beautifully spinning kaleidoscope of focus. I'm still alive. Then my hair was yanked, pulling my head back and, what is that? A gravy bowl? Oh, how practical I thought as my expelled juices were poured into my cleave gag parted lips.

To be this defiled and still I sense orgasm number two, a vicious predator slinking about unseen in the long grass on some exotic continent, hunting for its next me-al. Gee willikers, there's a whole lot of somethings wrong with me. I'm such a freak. A dirty, slutty, little freak. I'm so glad I'm not right.

A fair amount of me had dripped down the sides of my mouth and had kept flowing down the front of my body. As I was securing the last leg to the floor it was starting to feel sticky and drying a bit. Pulling and stretching my skin where science of things had determined it would finally reside. I feel so dirty, so wronged and so defiled. "Yet you feel so damn good about it?" Oh, it's you. "Don't deflect, answer the question." You know I do, don't be dum...

Veronica had interrupted these ramblings that myself and I were having with a hot pink collar she had draped over one hand. She sensually wrapped it around my neck as Mandy kept my hair clear of its new resting place. Veronica placed two fingers between my collar and neck as one would to check for an animal. Then finished with a little heart shaped padlock in the lockable buckle on the collar.

"It's about damn time, bitch" Mandy stated before roughly clicking a matching leash to my collar.

I stood and walked, as was expected of me when in heels.

"We need a second leash." Mandy stated, "so we can control her as one would using snare bars with a dangerous wild animal. You are dangerous, aren't you?" she asked as she yanked on the leash.

I was about to ask permission to answer when Veronica put up the universal stop hand motion in front of me. In her other hand was the multi-tool in pliers mode. Her next hand motion was a twirl of her finger finished in a pointing to the floor. I turned around and then I dropped down to my knees.

After she loosened the knot and removed the gag, I asked. "Mistress Mandy, Mistress Veronica, may I answer the question?"

"You may.

"Yes."

"Mistress Veronica, Mistress Mandy, I am capable of being incredibly dangerous. The only way your slave could envision my goddesses being witness to just how dangerous that is, would be if I seen dangers of any kind, or a threat to either of you. Mistress Mandy, Mistress Veronica, I am your danger to wield and order in any ways within the constraints of morality. No force on earth or in the cosmos is prepared for the ramifications of making enemies with either, or both of you."

15

It was taking every ounce of self control the man had. Sellkritch had made the conscious decision to stop looking at the time not long after his arrival on site. First, it was only adding to his rage and second, it was routine for Sellkritch. At any given time in an operation, he would just stop looking at the time passing. Why bother, you know it is still moving, stops for no one and nothing and though this relevance couldn't be denied, a pot of water on a heat source will boil over. So just react accordingly. Instead of letting the situation control you, stay in control of the situation. This methodology that had served Sellkritch well in his past exploits was failing him now. It was personal. Thus, the situation was more in control of his simmering volume, the personal, an unwarranted pinch of salt, throwing off the timing of his boiling over.

"Sands?" Sellkritch asked, now somewhat impatient.

The man nodded at him, his face read apprehensive. "I'm troubled by the level of professionalism. Our operative got back from the coroner. She was successful in acquisition of a copy of the official report. The two men were obviously dispatched, yes. But in the coroner's opinion, it was by the well trained. All injuries before death were without contest. Even the man who ate his own gun was clearly outmatched. No indication he inflicted damage to his adversary."

"Combine that with our knowledge of the escape from the bank. We not only know the girl has help, we need to be open to the possibility that the help she has is paid help. Some kind of professional contractor, or more than one."

"Continue." Sellkritch didn't like where this was going.

"Even though our data doesn't support she had time to facilitate and contract such help, there is the possibility she had insight as to what was coming. So, if this is a correct theory, which we can't prove yet, this has us at a disadvantage. Without better insight, we might be hunting contracted professional help. We could be dealing with an untenable situation if our quarry knows more than us. Even if she doesn't, it would be unwise for us to assume otherwise."

"Once prey knows it's being hunted, it's an even more likely possibility roles can reverse. Any actionable leads we follow up from here on out could be for us to see and for us to follow."

"A trap. This is a complication we don't need right now, dammit."

"I understand the inconvenience of it, but there is another way of looking at it."

"I'm on a knife's, knife's, razor's edge here, Sands. Out with it."

"We can't be lured into a trap without the act of luring. That act is what we need at this point. We have nothing else to go on. The trail is cold once again."

Sellkritch looked at the man. Largely in resentment but also equally in admiration. Sands was capable of such a vulpine nature, Sellkritch suspected he was born in a den.

"Sands, are you happy where you are?"

"Sir, I have no thought on it one way or the other. I'm not trying to be evasive about it when I say this. If you are currently happy with where I am, then I am likewise."

"You could have been a politician, Sands. Diplomatic, I am not. Let me say this. There may be a promotion of sorts in your future. You would have to want it though. Cut this, "'If you're happy, then I am,' horse shit. Just something for you to ponder on."

"Sir, I'm honoured. And since we're cutting excrement, I'll speak plainly. We both come out of this calamity on top and in good health, I'd feel like I'd earned it. But I'm only going to feel deserving if I contribute to the desirable conclusion. I fail at that, I need more time as a second in command before being ready for the leadership you are indicating."

"So your idea of leaders is what, they shouldn't fail?"

"It cuts deeper than that sir. Leaders can and will fail as long as the sun still rises. So the other will occur. Leaders worth their title are capable of turning the reality of failure to success. Make a win out of a loss."

"I'm not following, Sands."

"I know what's at stake on this operation, and I haven't the experience to see any way possible for it to be anything but one way or the other. We will win or it's a loss, a big loss."

Sellkritch looked at the man for a long time. He never had an heir to his throne. "Enough of all that. What's the play, Sands."

"I'll have our people reconnoitre the hotel. It's where we'll have our opportunity to be lured in. I have to ask something though, sir."

Sellkritch was stunned. He had never known those words in relation to the man standing before him.

"I'm listening."

"Hang back from this one sir, I see little possibility of it coming to a good end."

"Sands, I can't do that. I think you know why."

"Yes sir. I had to ask, however, in that case I'll be having some contingencies put into place."

"I trust your judgment, perhaps more than my own at this point, Sands. Do what you deem prudent."

Before turning, he gave a respectful nod and if Sellkritch didn't know better, an appreciative smile.

16

Being that my back was to them both, I had no idea how my sentiment expressed was received. But I meant every word. I also wondered if I just washed out the mood. I thought my answer came in the form of two hands, one on each of my shoulders.

Then Veronica spoke.

"I am certain there is no warrior walking this planet that is your equal, none matching in tenacity, fierceness or resolve."

Then Mandy spoke.

"No warrior is your equal, none matching your honour, courage or conduct."

There it is, I should have... wait...
Both their hands slid down to my breasts, each found their own nipple and clamped down hard. Oh thank you my Goddesses.

I stayed silent as the pinch of each grew stronger and stronger. Both seeming impossibly equal in amount of force.

Then as if rehearsed the whispers started.

Veronica in my right ear. "However..."

Mandy in my left. "Slave..."

Right. "Your..."

Left. "Skills..."

"As a..."

"Submissive..."

"Still..."

"Disappoint..."

Thank you, thank you, thank you my goddesses!

Then both grips on each of my nipples squeezed harder, twisted violently, let go and then both hands roughly slapped the outside of each of my breasts hard. They freight train piled up painfully in the centre of my chest.

I barely finished wincing when I felt the leash slack taken in, the collar digging into my neck and it naturally turning me around to face them both.

They both sat on their haunches, both held the single leash and both hand over hand pulled me to the water.

My Veronica spoke. "Drink up while you can, pet."

My Mandy added. "You'll be needing the hydration."

"We've decided to let you have water without earning it in lash. Because you are worthy of it." Veronica stated.

Damn..

"We've decided not to lash you in trade for earning anything." Mandy added.

Damn!

However Mandy hadn't finished. "We will just lash you regardless. Because you are worthy of it."

DAMN YA!

"Now drink, pet." They both said in unison.

It was freaky how they were so in tune with their domination of their freak. Me. Please let it always be me. I thought, as my head was pushed down to the water with two firm hands.

After lapping up a bottle and a half, Veronica rummaged in one of my excitement bags and produced a set of hot pink handcuffs. After being restrained with hands behind my back I was led to the bathroom. They both controlled my descent down on the toilet and then stood there while I peed again. If their impatient body language and facial expressions weren't genuine, Oscar's and Emmy's for the acting.

Wondering which of them would be folding or wadding up toilet paper for the dab dry was answered when Mandy produced my dish towel. Oh my goodness! I thought. She freshly spun twisted my gag, found perfect centre and controlled the tie ends with her right hand, reaching with the somewhat still damp folded mouth section between my legs. Her hand down there rubbing against both of my inner thighs as she dabbed me dry. It was a fool's errand. I was getting wet all over again.

Just as she came up with the gag and I opened my mouth, trying to look forlorn and probably failing to epic proportions. Veronica spoke. "Sister, may I?" extending her hand for the gag.

"Of course, sister." Mandy replied, handing both tie ends to her.

"Stand slut!" Veronica commanded.

I tested for balance and rose up.

"Face me and spread your legs!" She barked again.

With a tone of impatience, as if I should have known.

"We should really make sure she's dry," She said while she swung one tie end of the twisted towel between my spread legs. Having perfectly caught it out the back of them.

Oh gosh, I know where this is goi.. "Yiee!" I yelped. When she yanked up hard.

And as she was inspecting her work, alignment of where my mouth portion of the towel was, I saw her smile at Mandy who I assumed was also smiling, she then commented with a growl. "Deep up in there."

"May I help?" Mandy asked.

"I was just going to ask, my dear. Thank you," Veronica purred.

They both took what felt to be two-handed firm grips of the towel. Please don't tear, please be Egyptian weave or some high... "AAARGH!!!" I groaned as my heels left the bathroom floor. The only problem would have been my centre of gravity. Mandy had threaded the dish towel between my body and my cuffed wrists. Even in heels, both my goddesses had a few inches on me and I only weighed a measly amount. It seemed they had a good grip, strength to lift, position ideal and distribution of task nominal exertion.

They both moved in on me as they lifted, which resulted in no centre of gravity issues. I felt Veronica's leather corset with her pronounced cleavage smooshing my own unadorned breasts. I felt Mandy's clothed breasts push in against the bare skin of my back. And I felt my dish towel dig into me for all its worth. I owe species Gossypium the world over a debt unfathomable. And my debits are about to be added to! Oh shit! Oh damn! Oh my goodness! I needed to scream out words while my delirium was low enough that I remembered how to speak them. Three more seconds and I'd be too inept to say "cat."

"Mistress Veronica, Mistress Mandy, I'm going to!!!... my screaming faded off the second my heels touched floor.

"Yes slut?" From behind.

"Problem, pet?" From front.

"Nooo..." split second thought process, Mandy first. "Mistress Mandy, no Mistress Veronica, slutpet is as good as her owners decree." My vision was clearing, speaking was non-problematic now and memory was good. On the verge of a second orgasm usually did it to me. I've even blacked out a few times. Though the usual is that I would lose to a Mime in a linguistics contest and a gold fish in memory exercises.

"Slave was about to cum, wasn't she."

"Yes Mistress Veronica, yes Mistress Mandy, slave is trying, slave will do better."

"Slave, better."

"AAHHGgagchof!"

Mandy had reached around from behind me to capture both my nipples with little demon beast jaws hair clips and in mid scream my cleave gag was reinstalled. Tasting of me, my pleasure, my anguish and tasting of belonging, it to me and my mouth to it. What's a good name for a dish towel? Towelette is already taken, though I'm less concerned with infringement and more with lack of orig..

"CCCAAAWWWCH!!!"

"Slut, we're your main priority right now. Your mind and you can confer later."

"Ys Mistiss Vawanka." And she was right, I was totally unaware that she and Mandy had tied dental floss between the two clips. Dental floss she had just tugged on.

"Good r&d requires testing!" Chirped Mandy, as she disconnected my leash and collar, Oh gosh! Oh gosh! Oh gosh! and clipped the quick connect over the dental floss.

OUCH'IE'LICIOUS!

"Let the testing begin!." Veronica spoke, with a sinister chuckle pureed in with her words.

With that being my only warning, both my Mistressess turned and filed out, Mandy pulling the leash slack up and disappearing around the corner!

Shit, shit, shit! My mind mentally berates me. "Run dummy!" Click-clacking of my heels, my boobs bouncing, causing severe pain to my nipples as I think. One side of my mental discussions is showing promise as a dominant. Great, I start with two dominants, then I add a mental third of logic and now it seems three isn't enough for me?

We, all of us had reentered the kitchen and my legs went weak in sight of the chair. Nothing special about it, except it's taped to the floor and I can guess I'm about to be taped to it. I was painfully led over to it, made to lean over it with my upper chest resting on the back. Mandy wrapped my leash under the seat and draped it over my neck. I was impressed at how they coordinated because my chance of escape when the cuffs came off really wasn't a chance at all.

They brought my hands down to the chair, holding my wrists firmly. Then proceeded to duct tape around the back of the chair, passing the tape back and forth on each go around. Then finished with some diagonal passes over my hands, around my wrists to the metal uprights for the back. There I was looking down at the seat of the chair I was taped to, that was taped to the floor. There I was, feeling new arousal from within my nether region, again.

I would have preferred to be this restrained in the basement with the drop bars installed on the door. Screw it. Life without a little risk is whatever it is. But it ain't life. I felt severe pain as the leash clasp was disconnected from my little beast jaws that were left to keep eating in. Till they were removed…

"NNOOOHHHHOOOPH!!!" I gag screamed, then my hair was violently clenched. Nipple clamp removal, now that is severe pain, salaciously severe pain!

"What was that, slave!? Mistress Veronica asked.

"Yeah, did you just say no in our presence, slut!?"

"Yeph Mistis Mynde, ys Mistwis Vwanka."

"Oh, okay, no big deal, we'll be getting a lot more of that from you shortly. Right, Mandy."

"One hundred percent right, Veronica."

They both took their positions and I realized my ass was getting the break from towels that I was hoping for. Because the chair back was so close to my shoulders, my arms taped to its back on the seat side. They could whip from just off centre, top of breast to just off centre bottom. Which is how it went.

"swoo-SNAPSNAP!!

"PPHYYEEEEEEEEEEESHTBTCHSHTSHT!!!"

Both my breasts had a spot that was owned by bitch demons from Tartarus and they had hot pokers to play with!

"swoo-SNAP!!!

"SSNNOFFAABTTCCH!!!"

Bitch demons! Tartarus! All that on speed meth and crac...

"swoo-SNAP!!!!

"AAAAGGHHHIIIIEEEEEE!!!!"

Oh hell! I'm done with metaphors!

"Well that's six. How many do we have left?" Mandy asked.

"Well, there was the eight from before, four each, we were going to make eleven with the three for the water. Then our bitch messed up twice on our simple command of showing us equal billing respect earning another five from each of us on both occasions. You know, subtraction was never my strong suit."

"Mine neither, and we shouldn't go back on the three for the water before the rule change, we get soft and our slave could falter in her obedience. So, stick with the three, add the rest and start over at zero?"

Penetrate me sideways with a wire brush. You psycho bitches.

Veronica put a hand on my back in a mock, "I'm winded body language pose" and said "I'm in complete agreement as long as we add another two each for insurance if our math is bad or if we're misremembering. With a pet this badly in need of reform, we'd be doing her rehabilitation a disservice by underscoring what the little slut has coming."

Mandy matched Veronica, hand on my shoulder and wiped nonexistent sweat off her brow. Then she smiled and replied. "You know, when it comes to our work on this slave, I believe it in my very soul. We may never disagree on any aspect of what's of benefit to the bitch."

Screw you both. You bitchy bitches.

"Okay, let's each do our own adding. And confer on it again."

"Sounds good."

They both did some finger math on my bare back, tapping counts, some drawn numbers. I even recognized a four, six, a plus sign and a... heart? Really! And did she just draw a bloody square!

Mandy started to hum.

Veronica whistled a bit, the simple 1,2,1,2 345 from the good, the bad, a the, ah shit, at least they're taking pleasure in their wo-wait a minute, was Mandy humming the scary double tap from those shark movies, okay, come on!

"Done!"

"Me too."

"What'd you get?"

"I got 34!"

It was 31!

"Damn, I got 36."

It was thirty-damn-one!

"Okay, we go with yours but..."

"What's wrong dear?"

"Well, it's uneven, who gets last lash?"

I had just enough play from the tape to annoyedly tap my fingers on the seat of the chair while rolling my eyes.

"We had that bet."

"Oh right! Wait, who won?"

The potted fern in the damn corner.

"I don't remember, okay, round it up to the next even number?"

"Okay, sounds good."

Well, house of commoners-oppressors and Con-your-ass have done wors..

"You know, I really like your jacket!"

"Thanks, I really admire that dress!"

That's it, when I'm released, me and the Cuda are going to live on a deserted island and you bitches ain't inv..

"What were we, oh right the next even number."

Here we go, back on tra...

"So, 40?"

IT WAS THIRTY-DAMN-ONE AND YOU DAMN WELL KNO...

"Okay, 40, wait, add two more for good measure?"

I'm going to kill you both, cut you into tiny little, no, no I'm not.

"Are we in agreement with the forty tw..."

"Yes, I think that's best, 44 it is."

As I sigh in my own head, me reminds myself. Remember, you wanted this...

"I thought it was 46."

YOU DAFFY BITCHES!!!

So fifty lashes later, because they both found it amazing that twenty-five was their favourite number. I was drinking my own personal brand of salt water. Because I was crying into my water dish they had put on a stack of old phone books the on the seat of the chair. While they were over at the table, drinking wine and feeling fine. I'm not, I'm feeling divine on cloud nine. My favourite parts were in earnest a three-way tie. One time they both nailed my nipples simultaneously. Two, when Veronica gave up the secret of how she broke skin earlier that morning.

Mandy got mad when she couldn't do it with Veronica saying she was just holding back, they were having that contest on my ass cheeks. Veronica finally gave it up, "I dipped the towel tip in my coffee when you weren't looking, silly goose." So they got the rubbing alcohol and pre-moistened. I'll now have some edgy scarification on both cheeks. Three, was after they had reached 50, the two were taking pride in their work. "Look at the redness on this one, or this one looks like a such and such," as they'd poke and prod the marks.

My throat was going to be sore in the morning, fifty points on my body, more so. My legs burned, feet were in lava heels, my breasts, ass, and vagina felt as if I had wore a bikini made only of jellyfish. And I was crying into a pet water dish, occasionally taking sips. They weren't tears of sorrow, nor pain, nor happiness or even bliss. They were tears of all that and a cup of cream. Then my ears heard the words amidst their conversation, "forced orgasms."

And then, I heard a familiar voice in my head. "I told you, you're screwed!" Mistress Logica! Welcome back! How was your vacation? Oh ya, that's right, nobody in here cares! Piss off bitch and leave me be to enjoy this..

What fresh Tartarus toy is Veronica going to pull out now?

"See, with this harness, we don't have to hold the wand. Great, isn't it Mandy?"

Mandy leaned in to whisper in Veronica's ear. Then Veronica leaned back and exclaimed.

"I was wrong, so wrong and I'm so glad you are here!" She leaned into Mandy and they embraced.

Okay, now I'm worried, what have the wicked-bitches-witches schemed up? Will I be seeing evil flying lezbo monkeys any minute? I'm screwed anyways, I've clicked these heels tog..ohmygoodness! Was all I thought when they started with the harness and vibrator install and adjustment. Wait, why are they moving the table in here towards me.. They have me confounded! Oh you demented bitches, you wonderfully demented, demented bitches!

Four minutes later and I'm thinking, they could do this professionally, bill out like lawyers and buy Bill Doors by... next Tuesday? Maybe the following Thursday if a day or two were slow? Or is it Bob Gates? First name starts with a b and last name is something you open, close and can walk throu...

CLICK!"BBRAAWWW"

whogivesashit! That vibrator is AMAZING!

This is gonna be the way I want to die! I'll wanna live through this for more but heck yes! Forced orgasm'd to death! Tombstone as follows. "Here lies Colleen, may her genitalia never know peace even in death, sorry to the bereaved that hear her moans and screams still from the next life as they mourn her passing... oh-my-bloody-shit!"

"CLICK!"

Oh my goodness, they're going to deny me!

"CLICK!"

"BWWWAAAGGHHH!!!"

When the vibrator roared to life it would have had me screaming in..

CLICK!

"HAAMMUUBOOTH! PHWYDOTUNITOPH?"

Mandy and Veronica both laughed,

"Such an impatient slut!" Veronica stated.

"You've cum once today, now wait a few seconds and you'll get to do it twice more.
While screaming into us."

Into us?

Veronica came in with a cushion off the couch from the front room. While Mandy was stripping out of her dress.

"Oh no, if I use that cushion, we have to put down a..." she stopped herself and pointed, "trash bags, that cupboard!"

Veronica smiled, "Whoa bitch! You boss around this slut of ours, myself you ask nicely!"

Mandy started to blush and Veronica broke out laughing as she walked to where the point indicated.

"Sister, were our situations reversed, as they will be in an un-known amount of time, I'll be a tad unruly myself."

"Thank you, sister, truly, thank you so much for this."

Somehow I knew it wouldn't kill the mood and threw in my own jocularity.

"Wht awut eeh?"

They both started laughing and then Veronica having just returned with a large black trash bag, put her hand firmly under my chin.

"Slave! Our pussies mashed in your face is thanks! Be grateful!" She finished with a big smile.

Now I was more turned on just by the anticipation of this new scenario than all others previously combined. Into us, got it. Oh my lucky stars do I got it. Yeesh, I am so out of it right now, the potted fern in the corner got that before I ever did! KEEP IT TOGETHER, COLLEEN, YOUR MISTRESSES ARE COUNTING ON YOU, WE CANT LET THEM DOWN!

Wait, what? Who was that voice in my head, she's new. Mistress Potted Fern, is that you?

The water dish as well as the levelling stack was removed, the table position tweaked a bit and the cushion was topped with the thick black plastic. That smell of fresh trash bag will forever be a turn on for me from this day forward.

Mandy stepped up to the chair, Veronica offered her a steadying hand and as much as I could, I thrust my head forward in offer of another point of balance. I got a pat on the head and a, "Good slave," from Mandy.

Seconds later and trouble surfaced.

"No good, hold on, I need to shift forward a bit." Mandy said disappointedly.

"Just lean back sister."

Mandy did and Veronica pushed on her shoulders. Mandy's muff and my mug met with force but it dissipated soon after Veronica stopped pushing and walked around. They seemed to pause and contemplate.

I was just evaluating the simplest way to gag talk explain using the rope I purchased from the hardware store when my wondrous tormentors again showed me how gifted they were in these activities I'm sure they could do professionally.

"Veronica! Remember how much rope our pet bought at the hardware store!"

"SMACK!" "Ahhaa!"

Veronica had slapped my ass hard in celebration and cried with glee. And added.

"And I have something to anchor to for the rope!"

Tell me it's an anal hook, please, Mrs Klaus, that's all I want right now for next Christmas. This little girl has been bad!

Veronica came back with one of the wraps of bulk rope I had purchased and went to the excitement bags. Then she made me happier then Grinch stealing from the Whos by procuring one of the high end welded with multiple tie off rings anal hooks.

Thank you north-bloody-pole occupants!

Veronica came up beside me and also had the pliers at the ready.

"You're going to have to lose this gag anyway bitch, and you are going to saliva this up good."

As I took the anal end into my mouth and started working up the spit, Mandy's eyes met mine and it lubricated the process all the more.

"Good slut," she said

"Yes, such a good slut, willing to take one in the ass for the team." Veronica stated.

She removed the hook from my mouth, evaluated and nodded. Walked back behind me and spit some of her own on my ass crack just above the back door. So hot! She rubbed and circled her spit around my anus, getting me lubed in two orifices simultaneously. Then the insertion started and again my eyes met Mandy's. I gave her a grimaced smile and she returned a devilish smile her own, along with an adorable wink.

Oh good gravy, I thought as it spread me going full in. I felt it shift and tug as Veronica installed rope and then dragged out more rope. When she had a loose pile of rope on the floor, she walked back alongside me towards Mandy. Letting the rope slide through the hooks eye created a sensation sensational! And I moaned "Oh ya!"

Which provoked Veronica to yank on the rope. "UUGHH!!"

"Slow down slutslave!" barked Veronica.

"Ya bitch! I cum, then you do!" added Mandy.

Veronica handed the single and looped end to Mandy, she pulled hard and we both moaned. Hook hooking harder into me and my face pushing harder into Mandy's fleshy blossom. I'm dripping so much, I hope that vibrator is grounded! Then again, universe, 120 my pussy! See if I care! Veronica disappeared and returned just as quick, her arms full of cushions. She made and stacked and shifted them all into a wonderful lean-to of softness.

"Thank you, sister." Mandy half moaned and half spoke the words.

"My pleasure, sister." Veronica replied.

Tell me it's go ti...

"It's go-time ladies!" Veronica called out.

I heard footsteps, I felt the slightest movement to my harness, the less slighter shifting of the vibrator and then I heard the two most beautiful sounds ever.

"CLICK" "BBBBRRRAAA!!"

I moaned into Mandy, she moaned, pulling herself in harder, pulling my anal hook deeper. Veronica took position and made like a Lamaze coach, stroking Mandy's forehead and hair.

"You've got this, breathe, yeah, that's it, pull harder on those ropes, pull yourself into her."

Mandy's moans turned to cries of ecstasy, then to pleasurable screams, my heels were getting light on the floor. It became a tug of war between her and my weight and she was winning. The vibrator was cutting through me with its buzz, I swore it would dig in to my belly and keep going. I started to scream into Mandy's insides, she screamed in delight and pulled harder. I stabilized on the chair with everything I had while my heels left the floor.

"Hold that bitch down!" Mandy screamed. Veronica left position and in four quick strides was directly behind me, then rammed in as if she bore a strap on and laid down on me! We all screamed.

"YYEEESSSS!!!!"

And my face was saturated, her juices dripping down my chin and mine dripping down my legs. Then the whisper in my ear.

"One down, pet, one orgasm to go."

17

I reply, "It's yours for the taking." And then suffer genuine shock. My Veronica's look when she walked in front of me, was one of unmistakable aggression. I don't know what I've done wrong.

"You, selfish bitch."

She said, as she grabbed both sides of my face. I was totally baffled. Using my head as balance she put one leg up, foot on the chair. Leaned down and whispered once more. "

"I was talking about mine. You need more correction, that much is as obvious as you being my bitch."

I knew at that moment, I would go to he,.. wait, what's worse? "Purgatory." Ah, yes. Purgatory, thank you. I'd go to purgatory and back for this woman. Hell, I'd find an apartment, stay for an eternity and then find my way back for this woman. Whatever it took, whatever the cost and with no thought for myself, not one.

It was my second time at bat for the same picture of domination. Still anally anchored to my mouth's responsibility. Yet, it was undoubtedly all new in so many ways. Her taste, smell, the feel of her flower's petals rammed into my face. Then, there was Mandy's attentions, a Mistress devoted to her tasks, who I am sure was following a devious set of plans formed by her sister Mistress and her self.

When did they have the decade to dream up all this glorious torture for little old me. The bitches probably sourced all the needed components at the hardware store and built a time machine.

When we get done, I'll get 'em to go back 40 years and plant some trees so we can hang

a... SONOFABITCHMUTHEROFMOTHERS! Is that what e-stim feels like, oh my good gravy! I had no idea what she was up to, being at times three of my senses were senseless. My Veronica pulling anchor with my asshole for lake's bottom. My Veronica, only her scent I smelled, only her flavour I tasted, only her form, my eyes see and when she clamped thighs to my head, I heard as much as felt her moans echo off every cell in her body. And my Veronica's thigh strength! The pressures at the bottom of the Mariana's Trench would tip their collective hats to this lady's leg strength! I'm sure of it!

Wait, how many senses is... Who cares!!!

What I now sensed on my own body was some type of gel pad electrodes attached to my nipples, underside of my breasts and one was obviously snuck in under the wand head electrically grabbing my clit with every rush of current. The one that hurt the most wonderful was the steel hook in my ass. Electrified metal to sensitive flesh, inside and out.

At level one for system start, I assume, had me sending screams of eager spelunkers into Veronica's chasm. They would never be heard from again. I barely heard, "Next level!" It seemed to come through her thigh tissue into my ears and then I screamed louder as she pulled harder. I was on the verge, screaming and then the wand was cranked and the electricity turned up two more levels.

The miracle was I never blacked out, I enjoyed it right down the last bit of tracks. Up to the platform and then lost consciousness when the shoulder bars raised automatic. I awoke in the dark, laying on a soft surface. Couch, living room, it all came back and my hands went to places of arousal. My feet ached and my neck felt owned. They may have carried me to the couch and draped me in a sheet but they left me in collar and heels.

Bitches. Bodacious, brilliant, beautiful bitches.

It registered that there was a reading lamp left on at a distant side table. Even before getting up to discover, I mutter, "They left me a note, how sweet." I found my feet loving the ache then pulled the sheet up with me. I walked over to the side table, sounding out soft clicks from my heels and read the note I knew was there.

"We have both showered, and are sharing a bed, I'm sure you will make like a good little guard pet and slink around the house for a spell, feel free to join us but pets sleep on their bed on the floor. P.S. Thank you for the best orgasm of my life. You'll have to do better next time of course, but thanks all the same. You beautiful bitch."

Colleen smiled. If she scrapbooked, the note would be enamelled in the front of the binder, first damn page. As an afterthought, she picked it up again and flipped it over and found additional print.

"You really are weird, you know that?"

"No, you're weird." I whispered sibilantly.

Colleen hugged the bed sheet around herself, feeling royalty with some majestic robe and felt something else she hadn't for quite some time. Endearment, fondness?

Veronica woke, finding herself in Mandy's arms as well as finding herself feeling quite guilty about it.

"Hell with it," she muttered. Mandy stirred but only to stretch out, moan softly and then she rolled over. "Fine then, don't cuddle with me." Veronica said softly. Mandy made no sound of reply. But a sound of whimper like quality did reply from the foot of the bed. Veronica's heart warmed, she softly swung her legs out of bed and crept to the end. There lay Colleen, still in her heels and collar.

She held the sheet open and Veronica laid down in front of her. She pulled on Colleen's left arm, made a plumping action of her bicep and then made it her pillow. Colleen nuzzled into her hair, whispering just above her ear.

"Grabby bitch."

Veronica laughed softly. "I still want you to get clear of me. This time we have shared, Mandy, you and myself, it's been a fairy tale. I've appreciated every second but I don't want you or Mandy to get hurt."

"It's over."

Veronica sobbed out the words, "I knew it would end some time."

"No, you misunderstood. I found and wiped em all out while you slept."

"You asshole! Could you bottle the jokes, just this once?"

"I could, but I'm currently using them for something, like tools for a job I've never put myself to before."

"What job, Colleen?"

"I'm sure I should feel ashamed about it. The job is me concealing the way I regard you, the way I want to be able to feel, shit. You need to know. Veronica, when I say those three little words, I doubt I'm being myself. I guess what I'm saying is that if I could know it to be true, that if I said them to anyone and meant it. You'd be the one, I'd want that to be you."

"You're not making it easy for me to push you away."

Silence befell the room for a long time.

Veronica spoke first, "You aren't saying anything."

"All I've got are more jokes."

"Okay, lets hear one."

"Knock, knock."

"Asshole."

"Only when I'm awake."

"What are you when you're asleep."

"A sleepy asshole, probably dreaming of your cruelties and of shiny, polished stainless steel."

I knew she was stifling another laugh.

"Here's how it is, Veronica. If you asked me to leave you to your fate, I would. I'd hate myself for doing it, feel damned for eternity but I'd feel that and do that if that's what you asked of me."

"If you're trying to make this hard for me, congradufreakenlations you bitch."

"I can only be honest with you."

Veronica was crying now, her voice cracked. "Ya, I know that. You can't lie."

"No, I can. I just won't lie to people I respect."

"I'm glad you still respect me."

"Still do, right up until I'm forced into your vag again. Do you ever wash that thing?"

"Screw you."

"Like, do you take it for walks and just let it roll around in whatever it finds?"

"Fine, stay by my side and die."

"No place I'd rather be, shared activities are said to contribute to successful relationships."

"Time comes, I can use you for a human shield."

"I just remembered, I have to restring a banjo at my cabin."

"Nope, you messed that up. Now you have to stay by my side so we die together."

"Mission accomplished."

"You're weird, you know that?"

"No, you're weird."

"I hate you both."

"Morning Mandy!" Veronica and Colleen said in perfect timing and tone.

The bedroom filled with laughter joining the rays of the sun that had already risen.

18

The three of them sat at the table enjoying the warmth of the tea they all held. The chair was left taped to the floor in case of desired future use. Though no talk of such escapades had come up.

"So, what are we going to do?" Mandy asked, breaking the silence.

Veronica got very stern in her reply. "We aren't going to do anything, you have a son and an untarnished life here, Mandy. We may have succeeded in keeping harm from finding its way here and that's how we'll keep it." She finished with a look at Colleen, it screamed for Colleen to agree.

Colleen said nothing, took a sip of her tea and said more nothing. Both women looking at her expectantly. She put her cup on the table with great care, it hardly made a sound.

Mandy again broke the silence. "Look you two, I'm not a killer, I may not even be able to look at a gun but if there is any stuff I can do, I would like to help!" Her voice escalated, right up to the end, when she was almost yelling.

Veronica looked at Colleen pleadingly and pleaded audibly as well, "Colleen!?"

Colleen just sat there, statuesque. For almost a minute she maintained stillness. Though it was so short a time, it had such an effect. The two women expected to hear marble cracking when she nodded. It was so decisive, so slow and very purposeful. She finally spoke. "Veronica, hear me out. And Mandy, you listen well also. If we three were to start in on this, there are several ways I can see that we don't share equal risk. Some aspects of it could be almost none." Then looking at Mandy, she continued. "Mandy even if we come out of this winners, all of us unscathed and go on to live the rest of our lives happy and healthy. Could you?"

"Could I what?"

"I'm going to be a killer on this one, that's unavoidable. My past methods of leaving trash for the collectors won't cut it this time. If I needed stamps for that to work and sent you to the post office to buy them, you're an accessory just for buying postage."

Mandy was obviously looking at her willingness to help quite differently.

Colleen went on. "Then there is the hard question I posed earlier, could you... go on living your life happy and healthy? Think hard on this... you'll never hold your son the same again, never go out on a date the same way again and so on. I have killed before. It leaves its mark on you. No amount of time will ever wash or erode it away."

Colleen then looked to Veronica. "Oh, this means you too, Veronica. You may think that because you were born into all this means you're ready or that you know how it'll be. A person doesn't know jill-shit on how it is, until it is. No matter how much or little you play a role, you'll be part of that bloody tapestry for the rest of our species' future."

Both woman understood now why Colleen was so stoic before, a behaviour which she now resumed.

It was silent for some time, the shadows in the kitchen travelled. The sun beam from the window being both hunter and hunted of and by its own created darkness in the room.

Veronica was the one to break the silence. "I don't want either of you marking yourselves that way. Thank you Colleen, for putting it that way. Initially, I thought it was just the risk to one's physical well being. There are so many other ways of it hurting you both though. I know that now."

"Mandy was about to speak but Colleen just raised her hand and motioned, wait a sec. "Me first, sorry Mandy. Veronica, I have bad news for you, I decided to go after any of these people some time ago. To some extent even before we met, so before I knew of their specific existence. I know such organizations are around, have been and will be. If I don't see it, hear about it and so on, I move on, always have."

"This has to be said as well, from our first night together, I have only seen you to be more special. It's because of people like Mandy and yourself, that I look to these problems as if they should be mine. I don't completely shut myself off from the rest of my species. By choice I strive to hold onto my small sliver of humanity. So I can look at the darkness that others face and say, "I'm not afraid of the dark, maybe I can lend a hand, and you don't have face this alone." If I didn't hold to this, I'd become more animal than I'd prefer to allow myself to become."

"I'm going after them with, or without your approval. And you may want to give Mandy some credit. Maybe she can live with blood on her hands easier than living with see none, speak none and hear none on her heart. Just because a person may choose one of or all of them primates throughout their life, doesn't mean the evil ceases to exist. All that is necessary for the darkness of our species to overcome its light is for good people to hide their own light from the dark."

"I like my insight on it—better to trespass into evil, than let it trespass into you. Often, I feel I'm condemned to walking alone, along a damned path, living a damned life, my very existence being damned. I'm okay with that, but I think you both now know the ways in which I'm not okay with damning myself more than I may already be."

When Colleen went to reach for her tea, her hand was intercepted by Veronica's.

Neither looked at each other, their fingers intertwined and that physical link was something so much deeper. Then Mandy spoke, drawing both their sight-lines to her.

"Screw it! You know! Really, screw it! I'm one of those people you make reference to. I know what's out there, yet I just choose the blissful path of the ignorant. I'm no bad-ass but I'm also no longer that person. If I can help, I'm going to. And I'm not looking for your permission." Her eyes levelled on Veronica.

Veronica looked at her with thanks and a hesitant smile. "Okay, I guess we three are in, your top plan improved any?" she asked Colleen.

"Step one is know thyself, step two is know thy enemy, step three is knowing how your enemy stacks up against you and how to topple their stack. Right down on their damn heads. Mandy, this is your little corner of the world. If I needed three vehicles that can't be tied to you in any way. You have any thoughts? I'd rather not boost 'em from long term parking at the airp.."

Colleen was interrupted by Mandy's smile form. "Actually, I have a friend of a friend who has a used car lot."

19

Dean had issued the orders he'd received from Mortan. Tactics that were his to begin with. Two person teams, rotating every eight hours. He would have preferred six but they had one man down. He could still do kindergarten math but was far from operational. Pairs were near infallible, eyes up in multiple directions and one can roam on occasion. Then of course there's bathroom need realities.

Dean had personally selected the vantage points. They should be able to hold surveillance for three days without raising suspicion. He was grateful Mortan left such matters to him, it was the simple that could clusterfuck everything. In his experience he'd seen more operations go to shit because of the small stuff. Same guy or guys in the same place two days in a row can raise an eyebrow.

Dean suspected the outcome to be favourable. They weren't dealing with any unknowns. Knowing is the battle. He was about to take his shift on surveillance and was happy to do so. He needed a fresh pack and some time away from his charge. Idiot. He knew it was twenty minutes from their little corner of nowhere to the hotel and it was time to leave. Where the hell is Sammy? There was a reason he chose Romero as his second. A complainer but a professional.

Sammy stepped out the door of the old cement plant they occupied. No problems with being there, it belonged to the organization. No problems Dean knew of.

"Sorry, Dean, I swear I'm packing my own food on the next away opps. I still ain't right after that restaurant pizza."

"No problem, Sam," Dean said while eyeing his watch. "We will still be early. I want to stop for provisions though." The 20-minute drive after the pit stop was uneventful.

They set into position and text messaged Romero that they could roll out. As Romero drove away, Dean saw a car turn out of an alley and it seemed to follow. He was just about to send word of a possible tail when the car turned right.

20

Sands did not look forward to his next meeting with Sellkritch. Hating to be the bearer of bad news didn't really cut it for this development. He had a job to do and he was going to keep on doing it, an honour thing. Sands knocked twice and was admitted.

"How goes the wait on seeing our quarry?" Sellkritch asked.

"Uneventful, nothing yet, however, we shouldn't expect anything too soon. There's another matter I need to inform you of and it almost certainly guarantees complications."

"Why would I be surprised about that, this just isn't our week. Fucking hell." He put his face in his hands, massaging both temples with both thumbs. With out looking up, he beckoned with one hand and said. "Let's hear it."

One of the men was circling the perimeter we set for the hotel. On the pretext of walking a dog, he called me right away. He's certain that he identified a man he knows to be from another of the twelve. The turf war that drew together six of the houses last spring made it necessary to temporarily suspend some of the old codes. The one code being anonymity between the houses lower echelon. There was a lot of personnel sharing, myself included. So now a lot of faces that weren't familiar to me, or my own to others is no longer. We don't have that insulation anymore.."

"He got a photo and I can confirm, the man is an operative. From house Mortan."

"Gee, and here I was worried it was bad and it complicates things. Good to know it's plain horrible and rocketfuckinsciences things. Sands, if I thought you had one treacherous cell in your whole damn body I'd never say this. You have more news like this or worse than this, just come in shooting next time. Alleviate me of my misery."

"Sir, we may still have a positive in this. We may know where they're operating from. One of our operatives here on this op knows of some property that the Mortan house has in the area. With your go ahead, I'd like to send him out there with a second to confirm."

"Dammit Sands! So what if we do! Confirmation or not! Where is the damn positive!? Can you enlighten me for fuck's sake!?"

"We assume they're hunting for the girl, same as us. So we now look to them as borrowed men for our own ends. We keep a small contingent aware of their movements and we double our own manpower for resolution. It won't matter who finds the girl, it'll only matter that we make acquisition for our house. It's a risk, I know that, but the benefit is that we know of them, they don't know of us."

"Sands, there are two things a man in my position should never do. I've been successful in one of those all these years and only slipped on the other once. I think you need to hear this for the one day when you'll need to try and beat that."

Sands just nodded, but with immense respect and a glint of appreciation, of the gravity of the moment, in his eyes.

"Never admit to anyone that you are weaker than them in any regards, and never apologize even when it may be damn well warranted."

Sands stood as still as mountains forming, movement and development were there, just not visible under conventional observation.

"I'm now twice flawed in the apologizing and first time ever on the weakness front. I'd have you as an ally at the expense of my right hand, and I'd surrender a lot more than that to keep it that way. You're damn formidable. And my outburst earlier.."

For the first time since Sands had been working for Sellkritch, he interrupted the man. "Sir, I know that you would be an enemy I would not want. If I have any advantage over yourself right now, it's only due to the emotional investment you have right now. And you can keep your score at one and one on those faults. I ill-bred interrupted before you got the chance to make it two and one." He finished with a slight smile, then became his usual stoic self.

"Thank you, Sands."

"You are welcome, Sir. You have my gratitude as well, I may never get another, such as that acclaim you bestowed."

The two men stoically enjoyed their momentary reprieve from who they were. For that diminishing moment, they were similar, species Homo sapiens, equal footing and mutual respect. It was comfortable. The civility of it.

"You have my go ahead, do what you know how to do. If we have a chance of this working out, it's your insights that made it so."

"Sir." Sands turned and walked out.

Sellkritch had never belittled himself before a subordinate before. He felt no worse for having done so now.

21

Colleen had taken both ladies to surveillance school – change hats, jackets and even how to simulate a break down with the car you drove. It was half all the things you do to draw attention, the other half was to erase attention. A person looks in their rear view and sees what they are used to seeing, same as what's in front and on starboard or aft. Other cars.

A success in tailing someone is that's all you are to them. Failure is you're a car that peaks interest. Colleen's tactic of the three of them on a joint call, in three cars, with hats and jackets made that three times easier. Mandy had short enough hair for a silver permed wig. Throw on some old fashioned frames without lenses and she was an old bird driving a different Ford Taurus.

Veronica had her long hair in a bun and two hats with two sets of glasses. She was a gang girl with the semi dark Oakley's and a backwards CypressHill cap. The other hat and frames, she became a farmer or a trades woman with an old JohnDeer cap in a different Chevy Malibu.

Colleen was in the 2001 Dodge Neon, taking all the risks. The Ford and Chevy were picked for their colours. Silver and Grey. Two colours not well known for a benefit in surveillance, they blend in with surroundings and tend to not draw the eye as much. Colleen selected the Neon because it was a stick shift and because she had hurt one before. And like her, that little sedan took the punishment, the motor revving back, "Is that it? You can do better than that!" I have known every manufacturer of vehicles to make those occasional products that you would choose for a conveyance into a war. In the midst of chaos, its nice to hear the motor growl out "This is fun, is there more in store?" She had driven a 2002 once with high praise for the poor car. It didn't survive to receive them but it deserved them. She was flying around side streets and in parallel to their quarry, keeping the car in sight. Giving her accomplices time to change in and out. Cycle out their appearances, keep it all fresh. Colleen was a hundred percent certain that they followed the car to near its destination with those in it, never the wiser.

The car Colleen drove had received some quick modifications, no running lights when you turned off the lights. And thank goodness for stick-shifts, disable the emergency break wiring and you could slow the car to a stop with down gearing and the parking break. Which was how the three of them had arrived at an old barn a field over from the cement plant. Dark as night and unnoticed.

"This would be the first element of risk." Colleen stated, looking the hip roof barn over. It was a heritage structure. Not to be over estimated for its reliable strengths. Her girls were smelling of excitement, I've made secret agent monsters out of these two. All three of them were fit enough to scramble and climb up into the structure. Then Colleen showed them how they could human ladder to make it through a hole in the roof and up onto its top most peak.

I smiled, hearing their whispers of excitement and joy.

"I may not have had this much fun in my whole life," Veronica said softly to Mandy.

"Did you feel like a secret agent when we were following and changing disguises, because I sure did." She replied while keeping her giggles muffled.

I shook my head with a large measure of warmth. Daffy dames. The picture was soon apparent. Roving patrols, a main structure and several small outbuildings. I got a head count of nine including the two we left back at the hotel. Watching in vain. I noticed that one appeared to be not fully functional. But the rest seemed up to par and number nine was obviously management. He came out every 10 to 15 minutes to snag cigarettes.

Then because the other five of the six smoked it was fairly easy. "Bad guys that smoke, what a cliché." They could at least be professionals and wait for their smoke. With decent optics we could have got a head count from a high building five miles away. With the flare of light from lighters every thirty minutes. Colleen's merciless mind had already decided how she would take them apart.

Then put the pieces in some of the industrial equipment on site and turn em into kibble. Provide a public service and feed the hungry scavengers in the area. I could be a Nobel nominee. The only challenge she could see was how to convince Veronica to hang back with Mandy. They could throw on a scary movie, hand flirt eating popcorn, it may even evolve into a sweaty pillow fight. Dear Penthouse, let me tell you of my last Friday night.

"So what do you figure?" Veronica gently queried.

"Well, thanks to the help of my super spy apprentices we've run 'em all to ground, step two, destroy them all and step three we all live happily ever after."

"And the plan for step two would be...?" Mandy asked.

"Later, let's amsscray. We have pushed our luck with being here this long."

22

Mortan complained to Dean. "This is taking too long. I'm in doubt if your avenue is the one we should be taking."

Dean was already frustrated about being pulled off surveillance. Let alone just to be summoned back here to listen to a whiny and petulant grown man. Mortan had sent one of the sentries to replace him at the hotel and tell him he was to return to the plant. It was stupid, a phone call or text would have been more discrete. The man driving up and approaching them in plain sight was a blatant overexposure of the operation. It's yours with success, yet still mine with the slightest hint of failure. I may let you meet that bad end. But I damn sure won't lament. "We'd be wise to give it another twelve hours sir, if you're okay with that."

"I'll give it more time. But I won't give those who fail me anything. Remember that, Dean."

"I've always known you to be exacting in your leadership sir. It's a great attribute I respect."

Mortan smiled, "There may be hope for you yet Dean'o"

Dean was smiling back, while his interior grimaced. Screw the lack of lamentation, there will be a party with banners, balloons and a decorated fuckin' cake. "Sorry you're gone, now. Couldn't have happened sooner?" Now Dean was smiling genuinely. He excused himself with the pretext of checking on the protection rotation and to call in on the surveillance team. Got one of Mortan's insulting hand gestures for dismissal, turned and walked away.

When he stepped outside, he caught a man lighting a cigarette. Dean was less angry now, but the man still got an earful. "In this darkness, you can be seen from miles away when your lighter strikes! If you want to get yourself or others killed, then great job, keep up the bad work!"

"You're right Dean, I'm at fault on that."

Dean replied with a palms up gesture. No apologies was his preference but he knew his berating was about other grievances. Still, best to keep them on track thinking for themselves. He also respected that the man owned it. What was his name? Ah yes. Jason, new to their detail before their charge brought them down this perilous trail. A person willing to acknowledge fault is someone capable of slowly improving on themselves and discarding faults.

This new man, Jason had potential for being better, day by day. Impressive. "Hey, I'm an addict to the nails too, just duck into somewhere when you light up. And cup your hand around the burning end while it's lit. Now you know."

The man seemed relieved about Dean's being easy about it and pointing out there are better ways about going with things. He liked those under him to have a greater percentage of respect with a healthy ounce of fear. Unlike one little piss ant I know. Dean was just thinking about where to duck in to light one of his own when it hit him. The barn. He knew that Mortan vetoing the two person sentry detail on it was a strategic oversight.

"Listen, Jason, about the smoking thing, have you noticed the others being sloppy about it?"

The guy shifted uneasily, not wanting to be the group snitch. "Yeh, I guess we could all have used some pointers on it."

"No harm on taking the initiative Jason. Be casual about it but when you rotate into others out here, spread the word on it and the ass chewing I gave."

"He smiled, nodded and was about to move off when Dean added, and if you're asked. I'm taking a walk out to that old barn. I have to check on something."

Dean didn't wait for a response and walked off. It was a ways to go and he suddenly felt that time wasn't on their side.

After a ten-minute hike, he was just approaching the barn when he saw the shadow of a figure tracking off into the field and drop to the ground.

23

Sands had seen all he needed to see. It would be foolish to send two operatives back here. Better to have two men sitting off the road somewhere in wait. In the finality of it, he had decided to go himself. He just had that feeling it was where he needed to be. Sands was just climbing down into the rafters and retrieving his blade he pushed in between two boards for a extra toe hold when he heard it. The faint footsteps of someone approaching. He made the split decision to leave the blade, a four-hundred-dollar find for the next group of kids.

He could afford to lose it more than he could afford being trapped up in this old structure. It was the right call, having cleared the barn and made it to some long grass just as a figure came upon the barn. Sands dropped prone and waited. There were other ways to kill quiet without the implement I left behind. He watched in silence, even driving his sleeved arm into his face and breathing through the fabric for deadening the near inaudible sound.

The other man was also more than capable of patience. Sands knew he was still in behind the corner of the barn.

Both men settled in and took a long hard stare into the dark. There was no way for either of them to know it, but they had the near the same thought at almost the same time. This could be a long time to dig in. Time we may not have in reserves to expend. They also both sighed.

24

Sellkritch pulled his phone out when the chime of a text sounded. It was from Sands.

"Pinned down. Eyes on plant. Will move if needed. Will inform you of developments."

It wasn't bad but, it damn sure wasn't good.

At least it's him, any of the others and it would be more not good and less not bad. He's a competent operative, Sellkritch reassured himself. Leave it be. And he did, placing his phone down. It's a waiting game now. Ya, my favourite.

Sellkritch knew however, his team needed a leader. That responsibility fell to him of course, but he knew Sands had his own second and third in the chain. He picked up his phone, checked first on surveillance of the hotel and then sent a text to the next two in line to report to him. Now.

25

The three of them had been back at Mandy's for a while now. They had all agreed to no fun or games, they also all expressed mutual dismay. Mandy made coffee at Colleen's request. Mandy and Veronica now sat with Colleen in the kitchen. The plan was simple, one more trip out to the plant, but it was complex in everything that followed.

They were all on edge and ready to go in one hour. The longest Colleen was willing to give it, "We know where they are now. We can't know anything for certain later," she said while they discussed the plan.

The Ford Taurus was not included in the planning discussion. Better not to let her know she was expendable. It was nothing personal, but they needed a distraction. Veronica had already placed money down to reimburse the owner, a figure one thousand over market value. When the dust settles, Mandy still had to live here.

Both Veronica and Mandy knew their parts in the plan Colleen laid out. Colleen had encouraged all the questioning they could ask, she needed them to be one hundred percent aware of how things had to go. How they could end up going and what to do if all hell went to worse than itself. "After all, the distinct possibility of it all faltering is less than distinct and greater than impossible." She stated in her strange yet analytical way. Now she had to talk about the hard stuff.

"Mandy, we know you're not going any further on this, past the execution of our distraction."

Mandy just nodded.

"However, you need to know that it could come to it that you'll need to run, you as well, Veronica."

Veronica just nodded.

So far so good, Colleen thought. Now for the part that should be the hardest for me. "We need to all of us be aware of the consequences before going any further. I'm going to be off to myself for a while. Partially for my own routine of getting into the headspace for what's coming, you both could do the same or chat on things together. Though I can't emphasize this enough. What you both are about to do could haunt you for the rest of your lives.

Again, the two women nodded.

Colleen looked them in the eye once, then let her gaze drift to nowhere in particular, nodded and stood. She walked over to the counter and picked up Mandy's cigarette pack. Colleen with her back to them both, she just jiggled the pack as if the motion were words forming a request. Both Veronica and Mandy were surprised.

Mandy just replied, "Uh, ya, okay."

Veronica was more direct. "I didn't know you smoked, hon."

Colleen drew one out, tucked it in her ear and said. "Call it the optional for those who face a firing squad. If I was certain of demise, ours that is, I'd decline the blindfold. But not this." She walked out the back door.

Both Mandy and Veronica cast skeptical looks at each other.

"She's going to make it so she goes alone, isn't she." Mandy stated.

"Don't I know it. But for the life of me, I can't figure out how. I thought she'd try to drug the coffee."

Mandy spat out a laugh. "Ya, I didn't have any either. So, how's that sneaky bitch of ours gonna play us."

"If she hasn't already, I haven't known her to smoke in the near seventy two hours we've been together. Mandy, would you go out there for one, make her think it's your nic craving?"

Mandy nodded. "No problem." She quickly went for her pack and stepped out the back door. Colleen was just smoking as she had said. Mandy went over to her to get back her lighter. Colleen drew it out, both the lighter and the truth from her. "Surprised to see me?"

"Uh, ya, you got me. Wasn't sure you'd be out here. We thought you were making a play to leave alone."

"Oh, that's exactly the play. This is part of it."

Mandy's eyes went wide, Colleen was so smooth with the hand-cuffs that she only heard them ratchet first before feeling the unre-lenting cold metal embrace. She didn't bother yanking at her shackled wrist, having already seen what she was cuffed to. A length of chain going to the patio furniture. Which she was already aware, had been anchored to the patio itself for wind reasons.

Mandy got out the beginning of "Don't do this" before Colleen placed her index finger on Mandy's lips.

"Tell our friend that, if I have judged correctly she's already out the front door. Colleen finished over her shoulder softly as she rounded the house's corner, gone from sight.

Mandy sighed, "shit. Some one musketeer that bitch is." She re-signed to stay there quietly. Having already agreed to go no further than the little farther she was expecting to. Now it was out of her hands anyway.

Around the front of the house, Veronica had made it to the car but was having trouble inserting the key in the lock. Poking and bending down, she seen a foreign sheen to the key lock, is that? Glue?

"Going somewhere, my Veronica?"

"Bloody hell!" Veronica jumped, the voice she had heard had the coolness of arctic glacier runoff. It was so foreign to her, it could be a voice not of earth. It was her Colleen's voice. Though it sounded like Colleen, it had a cold deadness to it. Would scare the grim reaper outa its cloak. Shit, old grim would probably give up his scythe and lunch money to this bitch after hearing that. "Ya, I was, but I guess you knew that. Glued all the locks, huh?"

"Of course I did, my Veronica." Colleen's voice had warmed but it was still dammed spooky.

"When? You never had time when we got back... oh, before we even got 'em from the used car lot, eh."

"See, that's one of the things I would love if I could, about you. No joke, I respect all those things about you that one can and should love. Hey, listen, we have about forty minutes before I go do what I do, you'll be joining Mandy for company eventually. I'd like to talk before we part ways. Want to do it out here, or go join Mandy out back."

"Screw you, psycho."

"Get it right, it's a socio that I am."

"I'm not prancing in to play your little game."

Colleen walked around Veronica, exposing her back for three beats of the human heart. Veronica expected she was that fearless, no matter who, or what was in her milieu.

Colleen sat down on the hood somewhat hard. Veronica stood. Then she watched her raise her hand and point.

"You see that star up there?"

"There's a lot you bitch, could you be more specific?"

Colleen spouted off some numbers, jargon and something sounding like a weird title.

Does she actually know the official classifications of random stars in the sky?

"Anyway, it doesn't really matter, I was just going to make a point.

Veronica sighed. Then went over and sat on the hood beside Colleen. "What was your point?"

"Thanks for joining me. My point was going to be that many of the stars you see in the sky are no longer, they've already expired and our species will continue seeing their light travelling here for generations upon generations upon, upon. And Veronica, if you had time, the time of an immortal, it would be better spent, sitting here on this hood, until the car rotted out from underneath you."

"Then continued sitting here watching and waiting for that change of reality. The last of the light travelling to your eye, for your brain to process. Like a switch being thrown, click, lights out."

"Better spent than what?"

"Spending another hour with me. Spending any time with an entity that lacks the propensity for change." If I had my way, you'd get in that Cuda with someone deserving of you and drive till the wheels fell off, put another set on and keep driving. If I had my way, a switch could be thrown so my light you see, coming from a entity that is already long dead was switched off. So you wouldn't waste that precious time."

"You deserve better, kiddo."

"You don't get to talk friendly to me anymore, Colleen."

"Quite right, Veronica."

If they hadn't the knowing of the other's name, the last words spoke between them had the tone of strangers relating.

Colleen sighed. Took Veronica impersonally by the hand and they walked into the back yard. No real anything,

Mandy greeted them. "Uh, gals, what's up?

She got no response.

Colleen secured the other end of Mandy's cuffs around Veronica's wrist, in smooth seconds she had both ladies secured in such a way that comfort was still an option. She withdrew into the house, and seconds later re-emerged, tray, carafe, cups and bottled water. She set it on the table well with in reach, pulled out one of the pistols from her duffel that she shouldered and placed it there on the tray.

"What's that for?" Mandy asked.

Colleen was about her work by the end of the patio furniture. But answered. "Not all us monsters have a system of principles or rules."

Mandy had no reply except a shocked look..

Colleen dragged over the loose end of dental floss and let it travel over the furniture back of the patio furniture the women shared.

"With our ambient temp at present, that ice cube will melt sufficiently in 25 minutes to allow it to pass through that anchor eyelet. A spare key for the cuffs is in the cube."

"When the hell did you set that up?" Mandy asked somewhat hostilely.

"The first night we all came here from the hotel, Mandy. I can play three games of speed chess at once against more than capable opponents. Playing well over seven moves ahead and seeing the multiple variations of all potential victories, with ease.

"Oh. Well, what do we do when the cube melts?"

"Freeing yourselves would be a good start."

"I meant after that, Colleen."

"I know, I don't have those bigger answers for you. If I was to offer anything it would just be these, hapless platitudes and suggestions that they are."

"Live days that follow to their fullest. Tomorrow eventually doesn't come."

"Find happiness in all and with all those, you can. It isn't guaranteed either."

"Lastly, strive to be better than you were yesterday and plan for tomorrow on how you can improve on how you are right now."

At this last sentiment, Veronica snapped out of her stoic state, her eyes tracked to find Colleen's looking up at hers. Veronica's eyes looked near a meltdown of emotions, bottom lip quivered so slight.

Colleen smiled ever so slightly and in some impossible way at the both of them. The smile was that of all the nameable emotions, but it was just an act of going through the motions. If that smile could be described in words, they were of a dead language, never discovered and learned by modern times. Coming from a time perhaps before emotions were contemplated by the primitive of us. Our ancestors, who had no higher purposes than existence and to continue that, stay alive to be alive. Alive to continue a long walk on this earth. A journey most often undertaken alone.

And Colleen did that, after a quick nod, walked out of their lives.

When Mandy was sure Colleen was out of ear shot. She made a statement out of a question. "What could cause her to be so weird?"

Veronica again snapped out of catatonia as well as snapped at Mandy. "She's not weird! She's not what I thought either." Calming, she continued. "A wild version of us. A natural version. The version that has no problem causing another harm. Even emotionally. Yet she chooses to only do so when activated by a higher purpose."

"What purpose?" Mandy asked mystified. She was in the very literal, now on edge of her seat.

Veronica stared out ahead in the direction of nowhere in particular, then she raised her sight line to the sky, focusing in on a random star. "For survival, hers and maybe more importantly to her, the survival of others."

"So we're going after her, right?"

For several minutes Veronica sat motionless, with the stillness of mountains and said nothing. Veronica just kept looking at that one random star. Then the unbelievable happened, its light stopped appearing to her. Can it be? Veronica spent several more minutes looking at that exact same dark part of the sky. Optical illusion? Did I blink and lose focus on which one? No, I know what I seen... I know it, I know it, I know it! Only those that believe the cosmic forces speak to us, show us signs, or give subtle guidance, would even skeptically believe.

Veronica's voice sounded like the beginnings of a predatory growl, slowly transforming into complex speech. "Damn straight we are. That bitch still owes me forty dollars for a pair of shoes. I own her ass."

Mandy's smile wound up to excessive. Veronica pushed down hard on her thumb. The loud pop changed facial channel from charged happy to grimace improvement. "What the heck was that?" Mandy spouted out.

"I dislocated my thumb." Veronica replied as she slipped the cuff off with ease. Another loud pop sounded as she walked over to the ice cube, bent and picked it up.

"And that?

"I put it back in...place!" The last word was yell spoken at the final stage of having lifted the cube up three inches, then heel of her palm striking it back to the cement.

It was a bad day to be frozen water.

She walked back over to Mandy. Keyed her cuff open with practiced ease. Then with more of the same, retrieved the silenced pistol and went through the motions of weapon familiarization.

The slightest of breeze had picked up in the back yard. It was imagery icing. Veronica stood taller than Mandy had seen her before. Veronica's strange increase in height being more about demeanour than their seated and standing positions. Held low in her right hand a tactic black pistol, made all the more predaceous with the suppressor adding length. She could have been a vigilante standing high on a building's ledge, looking down on her domain and listening for screams of the innocent.

Then the voice, one of complete softness and so opposite the view, said sweet like, "My Colleen is probably only a minute or two away from that plant. Mandy, hon, I really need to borrow your car."

She didn't wait for a reply, Veronica walked over and smashed out the drivers side window with the butt of the pistol.

"Oh hell ya!" Mandy yelled, already on her feet and running. She was airborne and did a perfect hood slide on her tush. Hips angled up, lower legs clearing the hood scoop kit. Veronica already had the door unlocked and partially ajar, giving a hand hold for Mandy to arrest momentum and to aid her twisting legs perpendicular to the ground. She was inside fast as hell. Reaching for the racing harness when she stopped. "Oh shit! We need the keys!"

She barely finished saying the last word when Veronica yanked wiring harness out with violence. It took less time for her to yank and twist the wires together than for her saying, "What for?" The motor having caught before the last word died in her saying it. She burped the gas pedal half as fast as she had disengaged the clutch slamming the shifter into first and then engaged the clutch. The car behaved as a monster freed from its cage.

The Cuda's front end went light and lifted, the car a powerful creature, awakened and hungry. Veronica had the car at the street in another immeasurably short period of time and slowed for the perfect suspension settle into the low gutter between sidewalk and centre street. Veronica's handling of the vintage iron seemed perfect control of out of control for the extent of the trip. Destination, days to their fullest, to finding their happiness, and striving to be their better and improved selves.

Mandy hung in there but she wasn't tempered for rear wheels screaming with every corner and hardly subsiding in their screaming rage on the straightaways. As if by some strange design of fate, dog walkers were lazy, pedestrians and bicyclists had been removed from existence, and there were no other cars in sight. The route also absent of laws, orders and rules.

Police presence that was not present, had been pulled by unseen cosmic forces to the suspicious characters surveilling a nearby hotel.

As if a whisper could be heard, only by those that choose to listen for such things. A whisper saying, "Go forth. Your destiny awaits."

26

Both men knew the stand-off couldn't go on for ever. Dean broke first. Not out of any comparison of weakness or strength. Sands just had the upper hand, he was where he wanted to be and could have waited as long as it took. Dean wasn't where he wanted to be and didn't have time to wait around.

"You're trespassing, this is private property!" Dean called out in a stern loud voice.

Sands first reply was a cool smile. He doesn't know who's in the trenches opposite his. Protocols to follow.

"If I am, and if it is. So are you!" He called back and added. "The organization doesn't own this field or that barn."

"Shit." Dean whispered at the night. Protocols to follow.

Both men knew that. An unwarranted kill of another organization associate, especially from another house was forbidden. Sign your own death warrant, and it's up to your house elder to see it through.

Neither spoke again, they simply made themselves visible. Dean came out from behind the structure and Sands stood. They approached each other with no concern of their own well-being. Once they made themselves known, they couldn't have been more protected in the womb.

Dean pulled out his pack. "Cigarette?"

Sands extended his hand and took what was offered. "Only for diplomacy, thanks." He had smoked two cigarettes in his life, this one would be number three. The second was another rare encounter with another house operative. The first time he smoked was after his first kill. A smoke from his fathers own pack.

Both men held the cigarettes, neither going to the motions of lighting them. Sands twitched his head right and walked that direction into the barn. Once inside and around a corner, Dean lit the man's smoke and then his own. Dean took note of how the man held it, cupping the hand around its glow. Very aware of the simple things. Now it was Dean who twitched for the indication of exiting the structure.

"This place looks like a bucket of water could set it ablaze." Dean stated with conviction while walking into the open.

"It could at that. It would burn too well." Sands replied, walking shoulder to shoulder with the stranger.

Identification procedure still remained. Both men knew it.

Sands exhaled what he felt was putrid into the night air. "Thirteen boys, abandoned a sinking ship." He started first; it was only diplomatic.

Dean closed the procedure with. "Boys now Elders of the thirteen houses."

Both men breathed easier, taking some time before continuing. It was also death to utter the phrases for any other reason. Or the inability to do so. Even if a man had no knowledge of them, they were dead for hearing them or not knowing them. This simple fundamental that had kept the organization secret since those thirteen had swam to the harbour's shore.

Ball now in Dean's court, he would start introductions. Only diplomatic. "House Mortan. My name is Dean."

The only other house equal to his own. Sands knew that. He smiled out his reply.

"House Sellkritch. My name is Sands.

Dean was also aware of the importance of the random meeting of their two equal houses. Like he knew now he had to divulge his compromised position. But Sands made it easy for him. Though it was break in protocol, it was courteous of him.

"My house's involvement here is sanctioned and personally led by its elder." Sands whispered out the smoke.

Sorry Mortan, it looks as if your demise will be official. Dean thought.

"My house's involvement here is unsanctioned. I'm here at the behest of my charge, Mortan's son."

"It can be difficult having two masters." Sands spoke softly.

Dean had taken to his haunches to butt out his smoke discreetly, he looked up at a colleague. They may be from different houses but the Sands breathed out respect. It seemed it seeped from his being, it was a refreshing encounter after the last seventy plus hours of dealing with a spoiled piss-ant son of a king.

"Tell me something Sands. If you are so inclined, I mean." The fuckin' disrespect of his prior environment was taking its toll on Dean and he knew it.

Sands nodded.

"Do you see purpose in this life? The existence we toil in I mean."

"Purpose is an illusion, Dean. You may think differently and that's any person's prerogative. I believe a person either gives them self purpose during their lives or they don't. So if you aren't seeing it in your own, ask yourself this. What am I not doing that I should start doing and what am I doing that I should discontinue?"

Dean smiled, nodded and said nothing. This was a man he could follow, respect and give unquestioned loyalty.

More protocol. "What are my orders?" Dean asked. He knew that Sellkritch being involved in it all put him under the command of that house. He was for now, relieved to be free of Mortan's bullshit.

Sands replied. "For now we wait, contact being established between our houses means more protocols. Our house elders need to be informed."

As Sands finished, he removed his phone from his pocket. Then adding a sentiment of sorts before his call was answered. "We are mere foot soldiers to our kings, Dean."

Dean again smiled, noting how the man let no light from the phone escape into the night the way Sands tucked it into his coat. Dean wasn't an overly educated man, but he could agree with the nature of that statement.

Sands was now in communications with his superior, employing a tactical earpiece for the call. Dean heard the one side of the conversation and was fairly certain of the other side.

"Interaction between houses has occurred."
"No problems, Sir."

"That is correct, Sir."

"That's why I'm calling Sir. Nothing else to report Sir."

"Yes Sir, we will. I'll call again if anything new presents itself."

Sands put his phone away.

"We hold. When we are given orders, we will execute," he said with a coldness.

Dean nodded and said no more. The two men stood still, adding their count of two to the unmoving barn behind them. Professionals awaiting orders from their superiors. Like an old barn awaiting its fate.

27

Sellkritch and Mortan would be on a first-name basis, if they used them. In truth, no one knew them, except for them knowing their own. Those names were left behind with their past. Any who had known them were no longer alive. Their names and their history left behind with the dead. The House names used by the organization since the beginning were fabrications with less substance than smoke.

"I would rather not face the truth that my son is a damn disappointment to me. Sellkritch, you may have had the better notion in not having heirs."

Sellkritch was leaving that alone. I would rather vocalize a desert cactus out my mouth then speak on that matter.

"Mortan, our first loyalty is to the organization, our second is to our respective houses, lastly is the lives of our lineage, or even ourselves."

"Ya, I know, I know. If we see it any differently, we are unworthy to rule. The houses fall without the code. As we swore while the water was filling the ship. Before we swam, we all swore to it."

"Yes, as we swore to it. The girl, what is your son's interest in his pursuits?"

"He's angry with any that don't bend to his will. I've found out that much. I can only speculate that this is the same. Look old friend, if you can, I'd like to give him one last chance to be worthy of inheriting. I'm giving you a future token for bargain."

Sellkritch was surprised. Between Mortan and himself, they had never exchanged a token. It was allowed in the organization, but frowned upon. Asking for favours was showing weakness. Giving them was considered tolerance of it. The houses allowed it, judged it later and ruled on validity.

"Old friend, I can't promise a favourable outcome, you know this."

"Ya, I know. But without promise, token given. What say you?"

"I say this, between us, no token exchanged. Simply a bargain made, I will do what I can for your heir, within the best interest of us all. The girl is mine to do with as I will." Do we have covenant?"

"We have covenant. I will still regard this as something you can call on in the future. Thank you old friend. May I ask, what is your interest in the acquisition?"

"I have indebtedness to settle; she has been left to me to deal with. I will pay what I owe."

"I see. Well, I expect to hear from you again. Whatever the outcome. May our houses and the organization see millennias of survival and prosperity."

"It's duty we swore to all those years ago before we swam. At cost of my own life I will see that honoured."

"As will I."

Both men disconnected. All needing saying had been said.

Sellkritch contemplated what direction to steer things next. Sands had foreseen it. Our manpower is now double, making for increase of success twice the likely. If only it wasn't for the son. No whispers had ever been uttered. Just known facts. Any privy to them, knew Mortan's heir was on borrowed time.

He texted Sands to call. His views on things are what I need of myself. I made the right call all those years ago. Standing against all the remaining houses, taking in the boy and his mother. The vote was eleven to one for casting them out. Sellkritch was sure it would have been twelve to one if all thirteen still stood. Sellkritch had nothing personally invested and neither did the other houses. It was merely a complication of two houses involved in the incident. Sands' father and mother were of two houses. The incident had led to policy change. Unions would never again be allowed between houses. So such matters in the future could be handled internally.

28

Colleen had her timeline, she was going to wipe them all out. Not just the headcount at the cement plant. She was going to wage war, knowing survival was not a part of it. I will take as many heads as I can, make such an impression that this Hydra will see Veronica as insignificant. It will bring the fight to me...

It was theoretically possible. Veronica had told Colleen all. The man who had been turned down, felt wronged and that choice had made her life forfeit. Colleen had equal respect for both sexes of the species, if not for both, her existence would be a negative. But she hated men who felt their entitlement to females of the species. No, not hate. Hate led to the worst sins committed by one group upon another. Hate is too soft of a word.

I will take actions that will illustrate something far worse then hate. My conduct shall write in new language that which makes hatred seem warm and fuzzy as a teddy bear. First I incapacitate them all, then I paint a reality for warlords of history to criticize. I'm the kind that is capable of giving their kind unease to be associated with.

She was moving in on the first of her prey.

29

Veronica was on the last half of the journey, a long straight before the outlying industrial area. She had the Cuda in fourth, the pedal to the floor, hands clenched on the steering wheel. At top speed any car was fine, an operator was the problem. A shift of the wheel equal to a rodent's breath would be disastrous. She had several times now, downshifted and braked hard. Pot holes, frost heaves and one small bridge seam had nearly been both Mandy's and her undoing.

She was greatly regretting opening the door for Mandy. She was, as was her son, born innocent. Veronica was born into this evil, at twelve years old she was taught how to be an operator for the organization. Not the life her teacher wanted for her, but the level of preparedness that could be required some day. She heard those words now.

"You've been born into a pit, filled with vipers. Veronica you'd best learn how to slither, how to strike and how to bite, infusing those with venom that would leave you in their trail. Make sure you leave them in yours."

She had learned, everything from being Houdini's better to being worthy of a throne next to Ares. Her favourite teachings were how to make vehicles her own.

"It's not just your mind telling your hand to move to make a vehicle react. That's too slow. Inefficient. When you truly need these skills. Your hands are no longer muscles and tendons receiving control impulses from the brain, they become part of the circuit. Demand this thought process, give it validity, you'll be faster for it."

Veronica was approaching the next turn. Mandy was way over her skis, she wouldn't have been more afraid if she was riding on the roof of the car. There were times when she seen Veronica's shift movements a blur. Second to third, a drop back to second and then first. Once or twice she had blinked and missed the visual.

Right now she was looking at the roll-cage, gripping her harness restraint system and hoping engineers knew their respective fields more than intimately. She couldn't help closing her eyes when the down shift instigated a rear wheel drift. She opened them in time to see and feel the curb rubbing against the sidewall of the tire. In her rear view she seen the two mated at a forty-five-degree angle.

Veronica had a two lane street, width enough for parking on both sides. She took the corner so fast, she required every millimetre of width for the drift. This is nuts. Mandy thought.

"You look a bit green there, hon. It's going to be okay, I promise."

Mandy wasn't much better after hearing the sentiments from her driver that should be straight-jacketed and thrown into a padded room. "Ya, I'm... I'm okay."

30

Colleen liked to attack from height. Gravity is a very effective tool in physical confrontation. She had watched the two men meet at the corner of the large building. A very ineffective rotation. If they met in the middle of the long wall, it's harder to pick one or the other off out of line of sight. That, and sound doesn't travel around a corner well. Like Colleen, it just stays on course and plows ahead.

She was on the framework of a conveyance system that obviously carried material to or from the main structure. How the hell would I know, I'm no expert at turning desert particulate into sidewalks and paving stones. And three, two, ONE! Swinging from handstand position to right-side up again, both knees connecting perfectly with the man's face. He may be dead. If so, he is to be the first of many. She disarmed him and left him where he lay.

Her window for success on surprising the next man was closing fast. Meaning he would be on equal terms in the conflict. Aerial attack non-viable. Upon clearing the corner she saw the man's back. He was halfway from reaching his turn-around point. Colleen ran full tilt. Her steps in the gravel light and quiet. At ten feet she whispered out. "Hey!" The man started to turn at the same time he was going into his jacket for a gun. He never made it through the turn, and never made it for the weapon.

Colleen had piston'd her left leg from full bent on the last step to full straight. Her other leg was outstretched forward for the next hit to earth but it wasn't going to find it. Not before it found the man's wrist behind his jacket. The Armani provided no protection from the kick. It broke his wrist completely. Like smashing a sledge hammer on wooden dowels placed on an anvil. Sound comparable. But that was the loudest sound that Colleen's actions created.

In her flying strike, she had let her knee bend until her open palms of both hands had contacted his face. Left-hand palm encasing his mouth, the right palm found left side cheekbone. Her right fingers and thumb clamping down on both nostrils. If Colleen had concerns for his well-being, they would have been the self-rupturing of his own eardrums when his yell met her impassable barrier. She rode him to the ground, at the last second turning his head to full sideways for its introduction to earth. Head, meet packed gravel, packed gravel meet head. Oh, I think you both have a mutual acquaintance with a good friend of mine. Unconsciousness. Again the routine of relieving the man of weapons. Now I go find my next playmate.

31

Sands had declined the next cigarette offered to him. It was fortuitous that his phone silently alerted to an incoming call at that moment. He saw no reason to step away from Dean. They were on the same side, had the same orders and would continue down that road of cooperation. A quick glance at the screen of the phone inside his jacket told him how to answer.

"Sir."

"Put me on speaker, Sands."

"Yes Sir."

"I'm Sellkritch. Identify yourself operative."

Dean followed all protocol to perfection. He knew his future, either bright or dismal in the organization depended on it. Sands would be of the same mind-frame if he was speaking with the elder of house Mortan.

After the required identification process was out of the way, Sellkritch told Dean word-for-word what was said between Mortan senior and himself.

He finished with word of warning. "You and your fellow associates are under order of this house until relieved of said obligations. Failure to comply and the consequences therein will be left to my discretion...."

Dean replied simply. "Yes Sir. We are at your disposal."

"Good. Sands, our surveillance of the hotel is in good order. Dean, do a check in with your team now, on speaker."

"Yes sir." Keeping his phone shadowed by his coat, Dean dialed the number, the automated voice that came up did not bode well.

Sands looked the question at Dean that Sellkritch asked verbally.

"Have your men the sense to kill their devices before being compromised?"

"Yes sir. I have to report that they may be off the board."

"Unfortunate. This is the first you know of this?"

"Yes sir. Though I regret not having given Sands a full report of our activities. Not required by our protocols, but it would have been advisable."

"I agree, though we can't turn back the clock in these regards. So we move forward. If they are off the board due to legal complications, the firm will contact you specifically, yes?"

"No sir, if that were the case, when the call comes, it would be to my charge.

"I see. I'll have that amended shortly. Dean, I require insight on your charge. If you were in my position, what knowledge of potential risks do you have that I need to know?"

"He's an irrational and dangerous man, Sir."

"Noted, you will compose a simple point form text of potential concerns of dealing with Mortan Junior. I have covenant with his father to bring him back to his house safely, if possible. For now, you two continue to hold."

Both men confirmed and Sellkritch disconnected.

Dean began composition, starting with the most high risk concerns and would finish with the least. He decided to limit it to twelve. Finished the text with, "There's more, but these are the greatest concerns."

The piss-ant may survive to see a new day. Dean thought to himself. Sands shared Sellkritch's contact; Dean sent it.

Then both men continued to share ground and behaviour with the old barn. Right now standing against the passing of time was their only purpose.

32

Jason was on edge, hairs on back of neck were doing their level best. That effort they were dedicated to was to keep their host alive. An old trait, for when humankind was equally hunter as hunted. He wasn't sure what was going on, but dammed if he was doubting it. Something is going on. He hadn't drawn his weapon yet. Keeping his hands loose and ready was his preference. He had moved the tails of the suit jacket aside though. One side gave him clear draw to his Glock 19. The other side, his Trench Knife M3. Both tools had served him well, during his time in the military.

He was making his way back to the corner where he and the other sentry would meet. Then they'd nod, turn and walk back, looking into the darkness. It wasn't where he had planned to end up, working illegally with his background. Nothing ever goes the way you think it should. No matter, I'll be staying alive for the chance of better times ahead. Then, in between footsteps, he heard the slightest sound.

The sound of fabric sliding up against the wall, just around the corner. None of us would be intentionally doing that. We're on lookout, concealment tactic of backing into the wall is someone else's job. He contemplated all of this as he took the last few steps toward the corner. Could be nothing, however I want a potential someone thinking it's what they want. Me none the wiser and walking right into it.

She knew easy street just dead-ended. Dammit Colleen! For having backed into the wall without touching off with palms first. Wasn't really possible while holding the three quarter inch rebar though. It was about two and a half feet long with nice heft to it. Heft she was feeling now in her wind-up swing.

Jason saw the bar incoming. His hands already open and positioned central to his torso. He caught it with ease. What wasn't good was his split second of lost time. He was looking straight out from six feet nine inches of height. Once his gaze went down to find a woman near two feet shorter than him, he lost the remaining fraction of the first second, as he heard the violent little sprite yell in a whisper "keep it!" His training finally saved him.

Colleen didn't lose half a second when the bar was grabbed, just released it and sent her right hand and forearm rail sliding up the man's left arm. Her target was the man's nose, which Colleen's edge of palm found perfectly. After the moderate impact she slapped her palm down over his mouth. Then flexing her pinky finger upward to the eye, edge of palm under the nose she dug in the finger and pushed upwards. A whole lot of discomfort had her opponent kicking his head back to stargaze. Colleen's left went in for the windpipe.

Jason knew what he was about to receive if he didnt drop the bar. At the same time he did, he turned his face to his right clearing the finger from his eye. As well as the underside of his nose from the carjack-like force pushing up into it. Jason's left arm sweep to his right was more luck than training when it parried the hit intended for his throat. The block mutated into a wrist grab with his right hand. Now on the outside of the woman's viciousness he released her wrist and easily landed a right-handed punch to her stomach.

Colleen dug in for the fishhook but just missed the window. Seeing the next two moves, she just had time to clench up her abdominal muscles and use her feet for a slight leap. It didn't do much for relief from the blow. But she was happy with her current position.

Jason had felt nothing about landing the punch, just as he felt nothing about his knee coming up. Aimed to land in this violent pixies face. It never got there. The bitch slammed her open hand palm up between his legs. If that wasn't bad enough, the canine bite force squeeze that followed was worse. Of course he knew bending forward in pain was to be his downfall.

Colleen whipped her head back with perfect timing and heard her reward as much as felt it. She never stopped for banners and balloons. She also had no concern for the bomb site of a nose. Colleen wind-milled both hands into his face, left palm over his mouth as well as a repeat performance nostril closing pinch. Bringing her right hand behind his head and ferociously gripping his right earlobe, she then pulled with the strength of a Clydesdale. He proceeded to twist the way she instructed, back facing her, somewhat bent over, legs some-what bent. Her rapid two kicks with medium force to the backs of his knees had him on them.

Jason could sense the end, this bitch fought dirtier than toxic waste. He thought it stupid after he groaned, "Well done," against her palm, his teeth clenched with the pain. His head was wrenched back, a perfect view of the stars. Then a perfect view of his executioner. As plain and ordinary of any such women he had ever seen. The eyes though, they held him, – open tunnels giving preview to where he was headed.

"You weren't so bad yourself, big guy." Colleen finished whispering right before her knee impacted a nerve cluster she had learned about from a kindly old gentleman who's son she had saved.. She noticed he had something of a smile on his face, as she watched him lose consciousness. . It was more than his being a worthy opponent, Colleen sensed he had done very little, if anything at all to deserve a death she could easily deliver. You and I will talk later, ya big galoot. Small respects, like her easing him down to rest. Heavy too.

33

Veronica had been pushing hers and Mandy's luck, it was about to push back.

As Veronica initiate the drift for the right turn she yelled...

"Shit! Hang on!"

Mandy was already clutching the dash. But she opened her eyes in time to see the bad patch of asphalt. We're dead. She thought.

Veronica knew there was only one way to avoid roll over and did it. Redline, full throttle. Maybe. The 426 Hemi screamed in pain, the rear tires harmonized with screams of their own. It was gonna be close.

Veronica felt the rear driver side tire catch the least severe of it. By some design of physics, the tire jumped up and over. But in her rear view mirror Veronica knew it was over, for the radial. She kept the pedal to the floor. The blown out tire and its good sibling kept spinning acrid smoke. By the time the rear tires of the car were facing in the direction their cousin fronts had previously been, the destroyed rubber flew right off.

Veronica didn't miss a beat, with her shift to reverse or her quip. "Mandy, I owe you some new shoes."

Mandy, looking out of sorts, just whimpered, "Uh huh, okay."

Veronica went in reverse as far as the next wide shoulder, backing in left. Keeping the one remaining tire on asphalt and shifted into first. She could feel the rim degrading, she could see the cement plant in sight, and then she saw the Taurus's profile in the dark.

"You get out here Mandy. Check for keys, it they're there, give me a sign."

"Veronica I'm go..."

"GET OUT."

Mandy heard a coldness in Veronica's voice. She was still trembling from it when the Cuda rolled away. She stood there holding the keys, uncertain what to do next. She got in the car, put the keys in the ignition and sat there. Mandy knew it wasn't her responsibility, and she didn't have anything to offer Colleen or Veronica in the current situation. She resigned to sit and wait.

34

Dean and Sands heard the roar of a powerful motor, the scream of tires and then lower revving. They both looked at each other.

"Dumb kids?" Dean half asked, half proposed.

"I'm not willing to chance it one way or the other." Sands replied as his hand went to his ear piece to initiate the call.

Dean watched and waited.

Sands couldn't get the idea of it out of his head. The bank, the escapades with the blazer in the resort town, and now sounds of this nature. It seemed too much a coincidence to ignore. His call went unanswered. He quickly formed a text of his thoughts, sent it and dialed again. The result was the same.

"What do we do?" Dean asked.

"Stay true to our standing order. We hold."

Neither man knew what the other's thoughts were but they both had similar. Things are going to get bloody. If they weren't already.

35

Colleen was inside the exterior conveyance system and nearing entry into the building. She wasn't concerned about the fourth man at the front entrance. He could go and find the wreckage she had left in her wake. He could also alert those inside of their failure to check in with him on their roving patrols. Neither possibility was problematic in her mind. They would all be dead in due time.

They would all find themselves in her path of destruction.

Colleen had never allowed herself to go this far. She actually put blocks up to restrict it, knowing what she would become. Her blocks were in three forms. Avoidance. Routine. Apathy.

She avoided ever risking the encounters of such dark forces that she would be compelled to go so far as the current distance she now travelled would measure.

Exercised routine in always leaving the finding and processing of those she encountered that required dealing with.

And embraced apathy. In case her first two blocks failed. I don't really care.

Having met Veronica, it was as if she met a 19.9 world-ending earthquake, capable of shattering her little blocks. Along with the rest of her world. Colleen was honest with herself, she cared more about Veronica's continued survival than about her own existence. I just don't know how I could care about her in the way she should be able to expect. Up on the roof of that barn with them delightful dames, she had her strategy in less than a minute. She spent the other ten in argument.

That ain't you Colleen. What isn't me? Being ridden off into the sunset, Veronica in the saddle and spurring your sides? Shut up bitch, it could work. In what capacity? Her being honest about her feelings? And you being the liar about having them also? I feel for her! To what capacity? Getting pleasure from her causing you displeasure? Come on! She seemed okay with the truth. Oh really? Did you tell her about when your parents passed? Did you tell her about the exchange of those three little words!? Did you tell her how they tasted of bitter deceit when they passed your tongue!? No, no I didn't tell her.

Well then, what are you going to do next? Because you know, after all, I am you Colleen. No course is steered by this voice in your head, giving you deniability. So what are you going to do Colleen?

I'm, I'm going to leave her. Take her troubles upon myself. Finally unleash! Wage war. I'M GOING TO KILL THEM ALL.

Good girl, you go have fun with that. We'll talk again soon.

I'm such a bitch..

Colleen was up in the steel roof structure of the main building now, looking down at some distressed souls.

36

Being all of his past had led him to this point, Sellkritch knew what came next. Death.

His own, the girl, Sands, Mortan the heir...
"Who fuckin' knows..." He muttered to an empty room. "I know death is coming, but will I be okay with whoever ends up meeting the black cloaked figure."

Doesn't matter, he thought. I've broken the dam, reservoir of blood is going to flood the valley and we will see how deep it gets in the end. Too late to buy that canoe. He smiled, regardless of the outcome, it felt good to be in the thick of things one last time. I'm going to miss this maintenance of evil.

After reviewing all points of Dean's text, he had immediately ensured that all contingencies that could be covered were covered. Including the emergency medical Sands had already arranged to have on standby. They were set up and waiting in the helicopter. In his mind, he pressed an imaginary speed chess timer button.
"Your move fate, your move."

He never noticed the missed call displayed on his phone.

37

Veronica knew exactly where she would leave the car. A small lot with piles of gravel and no gate had caught her eye during their prior recon. She knew from past training from there to the plant on foot would take her three minutes or less. Now on her way through the dark, she found herself hoping she could spare those granules through the hourglass.

Call it instinct, second sight or plain old paranoia, she had left her extending batons gifted from Colleen under the passenger seat of the barracuda. Seconds after parking, she was off on foot, a baton in each front pocket. The silenced pistol was riding comfortably in the waist band of her pants, she was ready for war. If anyone kills this bitch, it's gonna be me. I'll hellaciously whip her to death and she'll love me for it, if she can...

38

Colleen had her plan, she was going to drop down a maintenance ladder, work her way to a back area with large hoppers and mixers. Then draw them in. She never made it that far.

Just off the ladder she turned to face a man holding his head, looking quite out of it and not at all capable of contest. He'll do. She eased his body down against the wall after having grabbed him by the nose. Pulling hard and by the time she let go, he was at full jog, head first into the steel column of the building's wall. Then Colleen found a random piece of dunnage and rapped it on a handrail. Trying for the force and sound the man's head would have made when colliding with it.

She slipped into the shadows and waited.
Her wait was not long.

"Dammit!" Mortan bellowed "Where the fuck is Dean!"

Good question. Certain I didn't take him down. She assessed that the man referred to as Dean was his second-in-command. Colleen had a headcount, speculative list and visual of each member of the group's hierarchy.

Big grumpy guy with playing-card black hair, The leader.
Stocky, chiselled out of granite guy near my height, Dean?

The rest, who cares? Bunch of irrelevant XY chrome dome's. When one really wants to win, start with an enemy's leadership.

"I don't know boss. I just circled the building, everyone is down. You think, maybe we should head for a car and get clear? We can come back with reinforcements, right?"

Mortan turned and slammed his open grip into the man's throat, started to squeeze and lift. Even with Mortan's size, his power was what should be feared.

Colleen watched. She was totally fine watching sinking ship rats turn on each other. What she didn't like seeing was the leader possessed enough strength to dangle his subordinate off his feet with one hand around his throat. I would not have survived this long without being a good judge of how formidable an opponent may be. This idiot killing his own man was more than likely going to be her Everest. If it's still possible for me to arrange the trip without a passport, I should go back and climb that mountain again.

Mortan finally felt the rage subside, he released the victim of his rage. The man slumped to the cement. "Coward." He muttered and walked away.

Colleen stayed in the shadows, listening to angry footsteps get quieter. "I've never climbed a mountain hunkered by a fire at Basecamp," she whispered. She crept from the shadows. Still crouched low, checking for a pulse, she found none. Death, in her wake, at her feet and waiting at the end of the path, Colleen started the climb.

Mortan was just arm's reach from the exit, when he seen a familiar face burst through the door.

"COLLE!"

Veronica got partially through the draw and through calling out Colleen's name. Her wrist was grabbed and twisted violently, the gun dropping to concrete. She screamed out in pain as her bones snapped. Then she was grabbed by both shoulders and thrown into the large building. Veronica rolled into it and came up wincing but on her feet. "Where is she? Mortan, what have you done to her!"

Mortan picked up the Beretta and smiled before saying, "You fuckin' dike, we would have brought it all to new heights. But now, I'm going to make you wish for death. You'll never see your precious little whatever her name is again. When I'm done with you, I'll find her. And I'll rape her while whispering your name in her ear.

Veronica felt hope, Colleen couldn't be dead, this bastard has never even laid eyes on her. She started weighing options. With a severe broken wrist, they weren't too heavy.

NO! Colleen knew that voice, what the hell is she doing here! She was walking dead slow until she heard her own name partially yelled. Then hearing her Veronica's scream and the heated conversation be-tween the two, she was now in a full-tilt run. Stairs, catwalk, flying leap through the air... Her perfect memory snapshot of the structure and all its interior playground. She knew what her course was and had already achieved ramming speed.

Veronica was fumbling with her left for a baton.

"What cha got there for me cutie?"
Mortan asked closing in.

He got no closer and Veronica only got her grip when the scream of all wars ever fought broke their milieu.

HEEYYY!!! Colleen screamed the loudest in her life.

Flying through the air, feet punching out before her, catching Mortan centre mass in the chest. He fell back into the wall, his commandeered weapon clattering away. Colleen had landed hard on her back, wind knocked out of her lungs, her right knee felt locked up from the force of the impact. And the bastard is still getting up.

"Heh, heh, heh. He laughed with a growl. So here's your little lezbo luv. I changed my mind, Veronica, I'll kill her in front of you. Then you'll be raped, me whispering her name in your ear."

Colleen may have listened to the cosmic voice, but she had never asked for anything from it. Until now. Tear me apart only to reassemble to repeat, continuous agony for the lifespan of it all. Just let me save my Veronica. She was on one knee, shaking when she tried to bear weight on the other.

"Say there bitch, by the way, what is your name, I'm gonna need it for later." Mortan said just as he grabbed a handful of Colleen's hair and yanked."

In the time it took to scream it she had thrown the reality of pain into a neighbouring galaxy. And pushed off with both feet in opposite directions. Her spin defying physics themselves.

"COLLEEN!!!"

Veronica saw a blur of motion her logical mind deemed too cartoon-like to have been a real event. The first scream, her precious

Colleen calling out her own name ripped her from the haze of it all. The second was when both of Colleen's fists landed in hammer blow against Mortan's left knee.

"Aaaahhhhiii!"

He cried out embarrassingly high-pitched and dropped to his own one knee stance. Colleen had completely reversed the previous reality. She stood, he knelt.

"Thanks for the lift Herc, my knee was a tad locked. Now up ya get, come on shitstick. We ain't done with this expedition."

"Fuck you, bitch." Mortan took two tries at it, finally getting to his feet.

The two of them started to circle, both relentless predators, numerous sunrises and sundowns of evolution and adaptation. This was a circle of life and death. Each of them having every intent to hold onto the former and deliver the latter.

Mortan's drug-addled and pain-influenced mind was finally putting it together. She went through all of my peons and only after first tussle with me is she limping. I ain't playing anymore bitch, gonna put you down.

Colleen had her own notions and thoughts, but, she wasn't at a whole other level mentally. She was above it all, looking down at the pathetic of her species. Still concerned with the importance of levelling up. How trite.

They both charged at each other, Mortan going low for a shoulder spear into her midsection. Colleen went high, literally, shouldering into a roll right over his back. Mortan's forward all-speed ahead combined with having no mass to impact and a sudden addition of weight pushing down on his back caused him to face plant, sliding on the rough concrete on his right cheek. The resulting screech of oily skin heating up to burning before being ground away could turn stomachs.

If those owners of said stomachs cared, they didn't. Veronica smiled at Colleen, and she winked back. Mortan only screamed in rage. To be expected, oh the males of our species and their self-endangering temper.

He seemed to spring to his feet as if the concrete floor was a trampoline with delayed response to his facial slide impact. He turned and charged once more.

Colleen was standing there in his path, actually evaluating her fingernails nonchalantly.

This time he was going high for a bear hug, and at the last second Colleen positioned for a shoulder spear but with zero momentum. Also with her hands outreached. At the split second they found his pants waist band and belt, she kicked her feet between his legs.

Colleen came through, sliding into a ta-dah! like pose on her good knee at the same time Mortan's mass smashed into the building wall. A satisfying thud resounded.

He again face slid, only this time down the wall. Veronica and Colleen's blood plummeted to cryogenic temperatures at what they heard next.

"Heh, heh, heh," Mortan chuckled. "This is what a man having the last laugh looks like."

He had rolled into a sitting position leaned up against the wall. Veronica's Beretta in hand and aimed at Colleen.

"And I changed my mind, she dies first, you get to watch." He spoke as the gun slowly swung towards Veronica.

Colleen had done the math, in less time then it took for him to say the first word. She propelled forward in a blur. One last balance of the scales, Colleen.

The silenced pistol coughed twice. Both shots landed in Colleen's midsection.

Mortan had seen her lunge, and swung back to her. Colleen now had a two handed grip on the pistol. Her left index finger jammed in the wide ejection port keeping the slide locked out-of-battery. There would be no third shot fired.

Mortan's shocked look and his repeated pulls on the trigger earned him nothing except a last look from Colleen. She actually drew out a cute batting her eyelashes expression and leaned in close.

Face to face, Mortan started to express fear, maybe for the first time in his life.

Face to face Colleen uttered, "You still lose," she leaned in further for the last word and whispered in his ear. "Bitch."

Her head sank down into his chest, he felt the grip starting to loosen on the gun. His composure came back in time for him to look up at Veronica, swinging some shiny black pipe into his face before it all went black.

39

Veronica had swung twice more, hearing the violence of skull fractures each time. And seeing the indentations of their severity. She stopped, tossed the baton aside and reached out for Colleen's shoulders. Swung her precious Colleen to be seated beside Mortan's seizing form. She grabbed the gun away from Mortan. Then stepped to the left, sitting down, she pulled Colleen gingerly into her lap, Veronica was entirely emotion, no longer feeling any physical pain and started yelling.

"Hey you bitch! We aren't done with each other yet!"

Colleen's eyes fluttered open, seeing into the eyes of her Veronica.

"Hey you."

"Hey yourself." Veronica sobbed.

Colleen's eyes went crystal clear, she surveyed the situation. Lastly, looking at Mortan's seizing motions, she forced out the words.

"What'd you say to get him laughing so hard...?"

Only when Veronica caught a coughed laugh and trampled it back down her throat did Colleen smile, maybe at her own joke, maybe just at gifting her Veronica one more laugh.

"I need you to do better than that and once a day. Have a good laugh, once a day, for me, okay?" Colleen finished with the back of her fingers on Veronica's cheek.

"Yes, laughs every day dammit! You and me will laugh every damn day! Just stay with me you slut!"

"I, i, i luv it wen you talk dirt to m."

Colleen was fading, but she kept on. "Ey, Im nt goin anwhe, I'm stain righ ere wth."

The door burst open with Mandy looking horrified. She had her phone in hand.

"I'll call an ambul...."

"No! Dial this!" Veronica screamed at her. Then recited a number that she swore would never be an option for her. She was prepared to die first. But not her Colleen.

"It's ringing!" Mandy cried out.

"Put it on speaker!"

Veronica was applying pressure to the wounds, looking at Colleen's eyes, they were showing less life after each blink.

Then the ringing stopped, the sound of the call being taken, a gruff, "Yes?"

Veronica screamed out. "Popo! I need you!"

"I'm coming child, I'm coming."

40

DON'TKILLMELOGUE

Sellkritch stood at a set of windows. They were not the windows in his office. It was no longer his office, then again, it never was. The house, surrounding outbuildings and the grounds were all owned by the organization. This is the life, we are mere stewards of castles and grounds, all this belongs to the covenant.

The houses had all been in support of his recommendation for Sands to carry on the Sellkritch legacy. Apparently "Hourglass Sands" was revered for his earliest work. It's funny, I never would have guessed that the eleven remaining elders only made it hard for me because of me. The one of us who had proposed it all. Who knew I was regarded as such... a threat?

Sellkritch continued reminiscing staring out at the blue skies, remembering when he first took the boy and his mother in after the incident. He recently found out that even then, Sands had wisdom beyond his years.

"I'm honoured to relieve you, sir. I've never forgotten my vow, the one I made as a boy when you gave my mother and I a place here: As this too shall pass, I will one day make it right. The debt will be settled."

"Sands, there is no indebtedness. There never was." Though Sands wouldn't be moved, his position was how he saw it.

Ah well. Am I supposed to take up golf? Go on safaris for lions, tigers and bears? Oh my.

And then there was the matter of honour and a debt outstanding. "I'm not cut out for this shit," he had told his equal.

To which he received the reply. "Then you best send yourself back to where you were cut out. And have them cut off or glue on more. You don't have an apparition of a choice."

Only man who ever stood up to me. He saved my life. And he's right, I don't have any choice. I wonder what kind of glue and cutting instruments they'll use, Sellkritch mused.

But for now he had some celebration in mind. His eyes cast down on a beautiful young woman on the patio in a handcrafted lounger. The matching one next to her was empty. "I'm too old for this shit." He muttered. He looked down at the tumbler in hand, two fingers of cheap vodka. "Lubrications for an old machine."

He set his free hand on the solid white gold door handle. Breathed in and out. "You can do this old machine." Then turned the knob and stepped outside; it was a beautiful day. He approached with care in case she slept, but only made it within ten feet before she turned her head. Looking at him through gaudy, yet expensive sunglasses, her smile brightened the already sun-baked patio.

Sellkritch moved to the lounger, sat and then swung his legs out. If retirement means more of this, I'm in. He swirled his vodka, sniffed at it, then rested it in his lap, cradled in both hands.

"Hello child."

"No, Popo, no, you know how much I hate it when you call me that."

Sellkritch smiles. "Well you aren't three anymore, I'm sure you've learned how to pronounce your A's. Hell, maybe you even know the pronunciation changes from time to time when they mate with other vowels and consonants. On top of all that, isn't Popo how rappers refer to the police? I'm head of a massive secret empire dammit!"

Veronica smiles. "You were head, now you are just a tired old retiree, I'll give it a few more years, we'll trick you into a retirement village and you can play shuffleboard."

"Do you want me to put a fresh contract on you Veronica?"

Her name pronounced with an aggression he couldn't make convincing.

It had been a little less than two months since the cement plant, they were still bantering with difficulty. The smiles and ribbing were genuine. However, fondness is a challenging mountain. To climb any peak without an understanding of it makes all challenges more so. And who in the universe understands love. And who in their right mind would attempt a challenge of such mind-screwing proportion.

He hated asking, but drew it from himself at least weekly.

"How are you holding up?"

"I'm actually doing alright, I won't lie, there are days when I just want to pack it in. Walk away from the table, cash in my chips, go build a hut with palm leaves on some faraway beach and... bah, I'll never give up. I owe someone a good laugh every day. If I learned anything from dad and yourself. Honour your debts."

"Good girl."

"Girl! Geeze popo, that may be worse than child!"

"Veronica?"

"Yes?"

"Shut up."

When Veronica looked over at Sellkritch, he was smirking. A blink later they both broke out in laughter.

When it died down, Sellkritch felt an open door and walked right through it.

"If you want me to start regarding you as a grown woman, maybe you start paying your debts on your own ya?"

Veronica smiled. "You remember how Sands always looked to me as his kid sister? Maybe we both go to him together, put hits on each other and see who is alive in the morning."

"Touché. After an amused pause, "What about dear old dad. Planning to visit?"

Veronica attempted a scratch under her cast and replied. "Yes, actually, the week following. This week a friend is coming down with her car that I'm buying."

"That's right, so you mentioned. You know, we have a genuine Superstock in our organization's possession. You don't have to pay..."

"We've been over this." Veronica snapped a bit harsher than she would've liked.

Neither of them apologizes. Shown weakness. The life—this life, it ingrains deep.

"Sellkritch swirls his vodka again, "It's your life, Veronica."

"Call me child."

"Then call me Popo."

They each smirked at each other. Then the sound of splitting wood drew Sellkritch's gaze. He pointed with one finger from his tumbler-filled hand.

"She really should still be taking it easy."

"Pfft, you try telling her. She insists on helping out around here. Couldn't train that one with all the newspapers in the world rolled into one big club. Besides she knows I'll only allow the quarter-sized. I catch her even looking at a full round for splitting and I'll tan her ass till it's purple."

Sellkritch coughed on a laugh. "Ya, old Horace caught her slinging square hay bales for the horses the other day. He said she's a difficult lady."

This time it was Veronica who coughed a laugh. "Please! I grew up around that old curmudgeon and he's never used the word difficult without an expletive preceding or following it to describe anyone. Come on, what did he really say?"

Sellkritch rubbed the back of his neck, uncomfortable with where the conversation went.

"Okay," he said, "she's a difficult bitch."

"Now that sounds plausible, she is a... hang on a sec."

Veronica raised a key fob looking device, aimed and watched as Colleen was setting sights on a larger round for her next conquest. Veronica depressed a button. Two hundred feet away Colleen's right hand went to her crotch, her left forearm across her breasts.

"What the hell was that?" Sellkritch blurted out.

"Nothing of importance. As I was saying, she is difficult bitch, but she's my difficult bitch."

Sellkritch shook his head.

"You two are a pair of freaks, each made for the other."

"Ya, ya... same time tomorrow, Popo?"

She called back over her shoulder heading for the property's large cottage.

"Wouldn't miss it, Child."

Sellkritch swirled the vodka he had yet to drink. "Her father saved my life telling me to dial back on this shit. Now I'm obligated to do so for my health to be around longer for his damn brat of a kid!"

He threw the liquid to the patio, playfully resentful, before muttering, "Best go find Sands, see if he has time to teach me how to make those damn smoothies so I can live forever. Damn indebtedness and honour."

***

I watched my Mistress for the entire duration of her walk across the lawn. Both appreciative and resentful, grateful to have so much time to watch her approach, resentful at it being so long to wait to be with her.

Veronica walked up to me. Reached up to my neck, playing with my hair in the way that gives me shivers.

"Hello pet. I hear you've been a bad, bad girl, playing with square bales."

"That Horace is a lying snitch, I never..."

Ugh!" I yelped as Veronica had aggressively grabbed my hair and hit the fire button again on the
E-STIM remote.

"You are lying to your Mistress. How much worse do you want to make it for yourself?"

I smile, "I'm hoping for real worse like.. sniff, sniff, did your snatch find a dead possum to roll in, or was it a skunk?"

Veronica smiled, then yanked my hair again. "Slut pet likes my stink, don't you." She raised the remote again for extra emphasis.

"Yes, Mistress Veronica, your slut pet likes everything about her Mistress Veronica." I watched her raise her sunglasses up onto her head. Even in that simple act, I see her being as important to me as life itself, my Veronica.

"You know, you're in for extra reforming when my sister, Mistress Mandy comes to visit... you will serve and service us well slut, yes?"

"Yes, my Queen, my Mistress. My Veronica."

The two look into each other's eyes. It is mid-morning and they both know they'd still be happily gazing into each others' very souls long after the sun had set. Even darkness would not stop them from seeing, nothing on earth or in all the cosmos ever possibly could.

ABOUT THE AUTHOR

Brenda C Dontcha is an avid reader reclusive type who confesses an enjoyment of reading her own fiction that her devious mind creates. A self-defined misanthrope and curmudgeon, though she still strives, ever relentless, to hold onto a hope. Just one. That we, all of us, every living creature, has enough tomorrows to work at being worthy of having them. Best strategy in that never-ending fray—do not waste today.

About the Author

Brenda Dontcha is an avid reader reclusive type who confesses an enjoyment of reading her own fiction that her devious mind creates. A self-defined misanthrope and curmudgeon, though she still strives, ever relentless, to hold onto a hope. Just one. That we, all of us, every living creature, has enough tomorrows to work at being worthy of having them. Best strategy in that never-ending fray—do not waste today.